STATIC DREAMS

VOLUME ONE

A Dark Anthology from Twisted Minds

edited by tara caribou

Raw Earth Ink

2019

This book is a collection of short fiction stories.

First paperback edition October 2019
Revised edition November 2023

Book and cover design by tara caribou

ISBN 978-1-7330808-1-1 (paperback)

Published by Raw Earth Ink
PO Box 39332
Ninilchik, Alaska USA 99639
www.raw-earth-ink.com

Table of Contents

Introduction

When night falls across the bedroom walls and your television remote slips silently to the floor, there comes quietly, shadows stealing in from the corners of the room and from beneath the table and dresser. Pausing, the shadows gather, then slip easily into your mind.

Perhaps your pleasant dream of flying across the hills turns suddenly dark as a hurricane rushes towards you. You swoop to evade it but are sucked helplessly into it. Yet instead of being ripped apart, you find yourself in a strange new place, a huge open room. A giant screen takes up one wall. In the center of the darkened room, a single armchair with a remote sitting upon the cushion.

Stretching forth your trembling hand, you lift it and push a button. The screen dims before coming to life. A man with a broken neck somehow stands before a room of people. He is speaking, telling the tale of his own death. You push the button again. A woman hands her despondent husband a Sam Adams bottled beer, several already littering the floor beside his feet. There's venom in her voice but his eyes are far away. You push the button. A man lays in his cramped coffin. Death apparently stepped over him for he lies there, his tie discarded beside him, as the puzzle pieces of a lifetime of memories, everything from office parties to first love, replay before his eyes. You push the button...

100 WORDS

by A.P. Christopher

Part One

One thinks little of the swarm of variables.

As much as we process and analyze, we never really see the world in that "big picture" format that we tell ourselves.

The metrics of mortality are so clearly marked. Delimited.

No one thinks of the devil in a fashion borne of logical integrity. This red-skinned, pitchfork-holding monster with cloven hooves and a tail. What fool signs a contract with something like that? Faust was an idiot. It's as clear a concept as the devil is transparent in his intentions.

But life does not push a contract across the table like some stern-faced lawyer, sitting there with some big ledger and a stack of papers. It is not when you are down and depressed, or when you've had a bad day. You don't talk a man off a ledge, or over it, unless he's on the ledge to begin with.

The devil isn't an idiot. That we believe he is takes my mind to the movie Layer Cake. "It is only very stupid people who think the law is stupid." It's that prevalence of belief that we know more than we do. It's a way of rationalizing how fucking brilliant we are.

When the sound came roaring, I didn't have time to think about it. It wasn't a deer-in-the-headlights moment. I didn't freeze and have some deep introspective moment. I didn't see my life flash before my eyes and see some old memory of when my grandma so-and-so bought me some cheap toy on a random Saturday morning.

I heard the roar of an engine. Tires tearing across the pavement like a fucking army running from a dragon. The only strange element at that moment was how compressed all the sound was. That weird doppler effect seemed to coalesce and slam into my ears like a storm of hornets with megaphones.

The devil isn't some sad trickster. He's not some slimy politician trying to sell you the idea that his policy isn't going to fuck you five years down the road when you're trying to decide whether you should pay bills or indulge in the luxury of clean water.

The devil knows that humans are weak and broken things.

The contract came to me in verbal form.

Standing there in a suit that looked like he'd been bargain shopping, a half-smoked cigarette in his hand and a plume of smoke rising up as he squatted near my body.

I could see the blood pouring out of me. I could feel the lights going out. The sound of my careless murderer as little more than an echo as the vehicle started up again and sped away with some part of the frame dragging on the ground.

The devil doesn't ask you if you want to sell your soul. That's the biggest problem we have as humans. We think that a question like that is something straightforward.

That same dumbshit mentality is what lets people think that cops have to tell you that they're cops. The world is built on lies by liars.

The devil, however, isn't a liar. He's just smarter than we give him credit for.

"Do you want to live?" he asked.

What a simple question. So basic. Ask it to anyone and they'll say yes. Those who say no don't understand the question. Those who are lying on a now empty stretch of city road with the pointy ends of their rib cage gently hugging the wrong side of their spine…well…who says no at that moment?

You don't think that life might mean disfigurement. You don't think about the potential loss of mobility. You don't think about the fact that you might be mostly a vegetable or not be able to fuck anymore. All that falls away and your mortal coil screams like a petulant child who has had their favorite toy pulled from their fingers.

"Do you want to live?" he asked again as he let his cigarette drop and crushed it beneath his sneaker.

Jesus, I thought, a cheap suit and sneakers?

My answer was a gargle of blood and broken teeth being transmitted on a tongue that was either swollen or bitten in half.

"Do you want to live?" he asked again.

The devil doesn't ask you for your soul. He asks you if you want to live. And at that moment, you say – even without saying it – that you'd give your soul for it.

You part your lips and between a small cascade of bloody mucus and pain so intense that you can't even tell what hurts, or what parts of you are even still connected, you say…

"Yes…"

Part Two

I stood before the mirror opening and closing my mouth. It's strange the things we get used to. It's equally strange what we don't get used to.

I get ahead of myself.

Often times when we tell our stories we want to tell the parts that we feel are the most important. In truth, they are often times the parts that we simply find the most powerful. Importance is a subjective thing.

When I found myself sitting in my living room, it felt terribly natural. You know that feeling when you drift off to sleep while sitting down? Where you feel – for the most part – quite awake, but in an instant, you have that one blink that goes immediately from awake to asleep?

It lasts only a moment, but you know it happened. It wasn't just a long blink.

That's what it felt like.

A trail of cigarette smoke broke me out of the belief that maybe I'd just had a very vivid dream from one of those more-than-just-a-long-blink moments.

"I…" I began to say…

"Shhhh…shh..sh..sh…" the man said with his finger to his lips. "I'll give you that one for free because you didn't know."

"I…" I began to say again. I heard it for the first time in that moment. A strange, sharp, sibilant sound snaking through my head. Like a strange, rigid coil of static was weaving around jagged points through my brain. A whisper of a noise like a TV on a bad signal but turned up as loud as an ocean crashing on the shore in a hurricane.

The man sighed. "Introductions then. And please, let me do all the talking."

He took a seat and put his cigarette out on the table top, fished out a fresh one and started smoking it, though he never once lit it.

"You can have a few days to acclimate if you want, but eventually you'll start getting those," he motioned to where my own hands were on the table. Hands that now rested on the top of an envelope.

"The fuck?" I said as I jerked my hands away quickly. The noise returned. I swear I could hear something that sounded like words hidden below sound.

"You really don't want to do that," the man said. "But that's how it goes. It's harder than most imagine, but maybe that's just how you people are wired. You've got a hundred words left in you," the man paused, took a long drag of his cigarette, "actually, you have ninety-seven left." The words came out with plumes of smoke.

I couldn't help but think of a dragon. But dragons didn't breathe smoke. They breathe fire. Well, smoke comes with fire. And dragons aren't real. A demon, perhaps…

The man snapped his fingers, "Right here, sunshine," he said as he directed me to look into his eyes. "This is important. You have ninety-seven words left. After you use them, you'll be dead. You'll be in hell. It's not negotiable. You'll want to use those words wisely."

I opened my mouth, about to speak. The man cocked his head to the side, his eyes saying the words "really?" even as his lips remained idle.

I stood and found a piece of paper and a pencil, brought it back and began writing. I slid the note over to the man who picked it up and turned it around so I could see it.

Nothing but a series of odd lines marked the page. None of them were letters, let alone words.

"Yeah," he said, "not quite that simple." He stood and snuffed out his current cigarette on the table like he'd done with his last.

"Keep a lookout for those envelopes. Keep your mouth shut if you want to live." He paused, his face in that pensive state like a man making sure he got all the items on his grocery list. "Yeah, that's pretty much the sum of it. I'll be back every so often to make sure you're still…you know…useful."

He began to walk away, stopped, and turned around, "Oh…" he started to say, "no. You know what? You'll figure it out…"

Part Three

I looked down at the piece of paper again, mouthing the words to myself but making sure that I made no sound. I felt immediately sure that had I tried to engage in a soundless conversation, the person on the other side would not see the words I was saying.

Everything about my arrangement felt like a fucked up riddle and I'd never given much thought to just how troubling life was when you couldn't communicate.

Stores were easy, of course. Put things on the counter. Pay money. Sure, I likely looked like an asshole now that I didn't offer any pleasantries, or how I gave that blank stare when they asked a question.

So many elements that I'd taken for granted had been taken by simply removing my words.

Well...not just my words...

I looked at the address and back at the paper.

3117 Harwell Ave.

That's all it said.

What does one do when they have no obvious objective? What would you do if given an address and nothing else?

I was effectively on retainer for hell. That's what I liked to tell myself anyway, though I suppose it was more of an indentured servant sort of arrangement. That situation works out so well for everyone in the end, after all. Then again, one could posit that all forms of societal structure are, at their very core, a situation built to...

"Sir?" a voice interrupted my musings.

"Hmm?" I replied absentmindedly – regretting having done so immediately as the wave of static and angry bees in my mind scattered through my mind. 96, I thought.

"Are you lost?" the person asked.

I turned to meet the gaze of a middle-aged man wearing the sort of outfit you'd imagine from a stereotypical suburban-dad type. Socks pulled too high, short-sleeved, button-up shirt tucked into khaki shorts. A clean-shaven fellow with hair that belonged to a mid-level office manager.

He was the sort of man that you could probably have a lengthy conversation with about push mowers versus riding lawnmowers.

I shook my head at him.

"Well, you've been standing in front of my house for a while," he said. "I don't want any trouble."

I gave him what I imagine was a quizzical look, re-examined the piece of paper and the address on the house and then turned and walked away.

— — —

Smoke brought me to my senses. It drifted through the air as sunlight danced through the drifting haze in that way that sunlight and cigarette smoke do.

"Tsk, tsk, tsk..." came the clicking of the tongue. The sound of a displeased father when looking at his son's less than impressive grades for the previous semester. "Was it too complicated?" he asked.

"I..." I started to say...

Fuck, I thought, 95...

"I'll make this simple," he said. "You're supposed to kill them."

He could clearly read the look on my face.

"What?" he said. "You thought I was sending you to tend their lawns? Make them cookies? Tuck their fucking kids in at night?"

His voice changed. He seemed suddenly darker. Ominous. His tone sharp...deadly...

"You want to rewind things?" he asked with words that hit like daggers. His cigarette jammed hard into my neck so fast I didn't have time to think. Luckily, my reflexes made me do that weird 'Ow, it hurts like a motherfucker' sharp inhale.

But then it felt like time slowed. The drift of smoke hung dead in the air. Then the pressure sank in. I could feel it around me like some invisible hand was squeezing. I could hear the creak of tendons, the strain of my blood vessels. My breathing was labored, chest tight.

Things began to snap.

There are no words to explain what it feels like to have the moment of impact from a speeding vehicle settle in in slow motion. Whatever you think it feels like to be hit by a car is nothing compared to having it inflicted in a slow, deliberate fashion.

I know I screamed. I don't know what I screamed, but I know I screamed. And I know I didn't just scream once.

— — —

When I woke up again, it was to a house that was dark, quiet, and empty. I touched my neck and found no wound.

Some might take that moment and chalk it up to bad dreams and a fear of repercussions, but there are dreams, and then there's what I experienced. It wasn't a dream.

In the night, with street lights and random wanderers as my companions, I made my way to a pawn shop. Had I known then what I know now, I likely wouldn't have worried so much. I wouldn't have looked around like a crack-head checking for corner mirrors and cameras. I wouldn't have felt so conspicuous asking to see the 9mm under the counter.

I could feel the weight of it in my coat pocket on the walk home. My hands clinging to the grip, fingers sliding around the trigger guard. Equally afraid of holding it as I was of letting it go. I wondered if it was what people felt like when they bought cocaine for the first time.

I sat there the rest of the night with the gun on my coffee table...looking at it, picking it up...holding it, putting it back down. I looked at the time as it drained from evening like an IV bag in a coma patient.

I looked at the piece of paper while the sun was creeping into my windows like a burglar intent on stealing my innocence.

3117 Harwell Ave.

Part Four

There's that phrase – "A blessing in disguise"

I wasn't sure how to weigh anything in my life. Blessings and curses, pros and cons.

There are times where the coin lands on its edge and part of you is hoping it falls the wrong way.

But I digress.

Thoughts like that are for later, and we're not quite there just yet.

3117 Harwell Avenue was nothing spectacular. A standard home. It had pictures on the mantle, pictures on the wall. An older woman that I imagine was the man's mother. A picture of seven people, none of them looked like the man who lived there, but then again there were a few kids in the group...maybe one of them was him.

It lacked more than it offered, though I can't rightly say what I thought I was going to find. A giant statue of Jesus? The Shroud of Turin? A splinter from the cross of crucifixion? A bazooka that shot holy water grenades?

In the middle of my thoughts, I heard the slithering sound within my mind like a snake made of hard bristles was winding around, spinning as it inched through my head. It had begun to happen more frequently since the night of my visitation.

How many words had I used? How many had been taken from me? What were the rules of this game? Were there any? Were they being made up on the fly?

The sound of mumbling brought me out of my thoughts, and for that I was thankful. A sort of blessing in disguise. To be taken from that moment of torture.

But then it was to be roused awake from a nightmare to find a dagger plunged into your side.

This particular dagger was named Kevin Arnold Webber, and he'd put up more of a fight than I would have thought he had in him. Maybe it was adrenaline. Maybe he was just a doughy, middle-aged man that didn't have enough fight in him. Maybe hell thought it would set a bad precedence if one of their little soldiers couldn't even subdue some random jack-wad in the suburbs.

Reasons and explanations aside, he ended up on the losing side of a game called "tie a man to a chair with rope and put a strip of duct tape around his mouth."

It's not a fun game. I don't recommend you play.

I found myself hesitating…for obvious reasons.

I needed to understand, even though I felt sure that there would be little understanding to be had. Even if I found something, would that actually make it easier?

If I'd found a holy relic, or object of divine providence, would it really have allowed me to justify killing him? At the end of the day, he was still going to be a casualty because he was on this side of a line, and I was on the other. I was a bullet in another man's gun trying desperately to rationalize why I was speeding toward his forehead so that I didn't have to feel bad about exiting with his brain matter trailing behind me like the tail of a comet.

Words can't explain the depth of fear and remorse when you're standing there with a knife trying to make yourself kill another person. A person you don't know. A person who, by all rights, has no need to die. All the while knowing that if they live…

So you mull over how to do it. If you have to kill, at least be humane, right? Make it painless. Is there such a way?

All those movies and TV shows make it seem like little more than flipping a switch. A stab here, or a few pills of this or that and hey, presto…they're dead. It's so quick. It's so easy. It looks painless. Almost gentle. A blessing, really. A blessing in disguise.

Wouldn't he be better off? No bills or job to worry about. Maybe he's alone here because he had a wife and she left him. I'd be sparing him the journey through a cruel world.

He looked at me with eyes that said "Please don't" even while his mouth moaned and mumbled words that were little more than strings of random vowels.

Tears soaked my own hands making my grip on the kitchen knife all the more precarious.

I remember sitting there with the blood of his arterial spray on my hands and clothes, tears streaming for what I'd done. Part of me wanting to scream and curse, to burn through my words and just let it be done.

But as people go, we're often bigger cowards than we'd like to admit. But then, we're also contradictions. People who want to let go but can't stop holding on.

When the door opened, I didn't even think to look. I didn't care. I didn't want to know.

Until I heard the voice…

The small, shaking voice that said, "Dad?"

There are times in life that we are given decisions. Terrible decisions. We must figure out who and what we are and hold to that moment like driftwood in a raging ocean. We must weather that given storm and hope we make it to land. All the while, we find ourselves wondering if we'll step upon the shore as something better than we were before.

It didn't take long to hear the sirens.

Part Five

Even having had that initial suspicion, it hadn't really registered.

The simple interactions were held behind the fog of my own transition. The differences were noted but set to the side in the obvious face of the facts that I was coping with an existence devoid of speech.

I, as so many are prone to do, looked for what was there. I looked for what I wanted to find…for what filled in the blanks for the questions I wanted to answer. I didn't pay enough attention to what wasn't there.

All those small moments.

Even had it occurred to me – the gravity of how eyes lingered or didn't, the way that words had been spoken, or not – I would have never guessed that it meant what it actually did. Not nearly to the full extent.

So when I sat there silently, blood-stained hands with inky fingertips, two cops sitting across from me, the sad revelation of reality was some illusive entity. As substantial as the men behind the two-way mirror that I couldn't see, but that I knew must likely be there – and so just as difficult to see or recognize.

If you've never been interrogated by the police, allow me to give you a quick breakdown of how this works. First and foremost, there is no good cop, bad cop; there are just cops trying to make you believe that they're on your side.

Phrases like, "You're gonna wanna get out in front of this, ya know?" "Being open and honest builds credibility. Judge sees that you told us the truth about what happened, it goes a long way to a better end result."

Getting you to confess for the sake of confessing is an art form. No one cares if you're innocent. If you don't put your hands in their cuffs, they have to actually do their job and figure out how to put them on themselves.

I remained silent. The irony, of course, is that any good lawyer would have told me to do just that, and had it been…I don't even know how much earlier…I might have found myself grabbing their kindly offered shovel and digging my own grave. "You dig it yourself, you can make it so it's just the way you like it…maybe put in room for a minifridge…"

Time stretched as they pressed me. They had me dead to rights, so part of me couldn't understand what the fuss was about. You find a man dead and another man in the house, covered in blood, holding the knife. You can't get any more of a round peg – round hole scenario.

But things weren't as simple as they seemed in my new reality.

When one of the detectives excused himself, I chalked it up to them trying some new angle. Go out so the other one could let me know that he was really on my side, but his partner…

Maybe the other would come back in with some obvious piece of evidence. Hold it up like a soiled doormat to a dog that had just pissed on it. "You see this? See it? You did this!"

I just hung my head.

Part of me wanted what was coming.

It was a dark, terrible train that billowed black smoke. It was coming right for me, lights shining so bright it hurt. All I wanted to do was lie down on the tracks and let it take me. Would it really be so bad? What use could I be in such a place?

It might have been the closest thing to salvation I could hope for.

But then the detective returned, walked over and leaned down to the other and whispered something.

They whispered back and forth for a moment.

"Bullshit…" one said.

They both left.

I expected him to enter. Some deus ex machina – pardon the irony – like Saul Goodman showing up to bail out Jessie Pinkman. In his possession, some file that pulled all the right strings in all the right directions.

But no…

Fate is a cruel beast. A monster. And hell is not so simple a master.

Looking back, I should have noticed how the cashiers didn't have the same look. The way that people who I'd seen before – seen so often that there was an air of recognition – didn't quite act the same.

I assumed it was situational.

But now the words echoed. "You know what? You'll figure it out..."

As they marched me out of the room and held me in place, hands cuffed behind my back. The boy stood there, a tear-streaked face.

"This man," the detective said. "You saw this man when you came home." It wasn't given as a question.

The boy just shook his head.

The other detective knelt down, and I could tell what was being said even without hearing the words. "Did someone threaten you? You don't have to be afraid, we can protect you..."

He shook his head again.

I looked to the side and found what little reflection of myself I could in a small bit of glass in an office door. To me, nothing had changed. I was still the me I'd always been. I had the sudden, unsettling fear that I had no idea who I was to the rest of the world. What face did they see? What fingerprints were my hands wearing?

Seventy-two hours later I was allowed to leave for lack of evidence. My fingerprints didn't even match those at the crime scene.

I returned home like a man who had lain down on the railroad tracks and found that, by some odd circumstance, the train had merely gone over me and never made contact. I didn't know if I was relieved or worried. Afraid or elated.

The answer came quickly enough.

The sharp scent of cigarette smoke met me on entry, along with what was – at that moment – the most ominous phrase I could have heard.

"You and I need to have a little talk..."

Part Six

I never knew much in the way of coming home. Not in the way that I feel like other people mean it.

When others say it, it seems to imply there's someone there.

My youth had been spent coming home to a house that was often silent. Empty in its own odd way, even when people were there. I was never really home…even when I was there.

It was a world of strangers living mutually. A shared existence with basic, civil pleasantries to connect all the dots so that the string spelled out the word "family" in about the same way as the constellation for Cancer actually looks like a fucking crab.

Years later, my time had been spent alone.

I feel like I can always remember all the people that left, but none that stayed there waiting.

Whatever sorrow those thoughts might have normally instilled, they were crushed immediately by who was waiting this time.

I could hear the cigarette grind into my table even from the living room. I walked in like a dog that'd beaten too many times but also knew when to come when commanded.

My kitchen table wore a slew of burns like pyromaniac polka dots. I couldn't remember how there'd gotten to be so many. Even looking around my home, things seemed…off. As though time had shot forward without me knowing about it. I looked outside through a window and it looked much the same as it had when I'd entered.

"Sit," he said.

I moved, but slowly.

"Sit. The fuck. Down." he said with the tone of a man who would not say it a third time.

I sat, head down, eyes averted.

"I like to save this talk," he said casually as he pressed another cigarette into the table, though I never recalled him lighting it. "I've found that if I say too much too soon, everything gets fucked up. Better to let them wander out into the world and step in shit before I tell them to watch where they're walking. They come back, shit on their shoes, and they have this look like I set them up to fail. You think I set you up to fail?"

I shook my head, but never looked up.

"Of course you do. But now we can have our little heart to heart. We can answer some of those questions that you want to ask but you can't because you're like that guy in the Matrix when the agent gets him into interrogation," he blew out a billow of smoke, "I mean, not literally. You still have a mouth. Kevin something..."

I looked up at that.

"Here's the abridged version. First, no, I'm not the devil. You think Bill Gates is still giving interviews? No. He isn't. Secondly," he stood up from the couch and walked toward the flat screen TV, his reflection barely visible under the dust.

I put my hands down as if I were falling, fingers sinking into soft cushions in the recliner. I had no idea when we'd changed rooms.

"You're not a superhero. It's fifty-fifty. Get these idiots that think they're that guy from Die Hard or that lady from the vampire movie. The one that always wears the leather...brunette..."

"Kate Beckinsale," I said...regrettably. The static was worse than before. It physically hurt this time, like a tumbleweed made of syringes and ball bearings was rolling around inside a skull made of rusted metal.

"ot ko atni mod ve," the static seemed to say. A slurred and grinding sound like a snake speaking latin through a walkie talkie.

"Third, there's no winning, and trying to game the system doesn't work. You think you're the only one that thought he could ride this out in a cell?"

He took a sip of his coffee while the waitress walked away.

The diner was sparse, a few random people scattered in booths and on barstools. The smell of cigarettes and cheap coffee as thick as perfume on a hooker before her first John.

"Fourth. No one knows you. No one ever will. This face isn't yours."

He was shoving a cigarette into the kitchen table. The whole top was more burn mark than glossy wood. I was standing by the doorway, the world outside looked so much like it did before I'd entered.

"Fifth, and this is the most important thing of all," he said with his hand on the doorknob. I watched him in his delayed departure from the table where a crumpled-up cigarette let off phantom lines of old smoke from its freshly terminated life. "Everyone thinks it's about the big fish."

When I looked down I saw an envelope on a table that had seen better days. The sort of thing that should have been hauled off to a dump three yard sales ago. Some piece of refuse in a house that only a homeless man would be squatting in.

I couldn't remember when I'd gotten there. I knew I needed to get home.

I opened the envelope as I walked the dark city streets. The light was sharp enough that I could read the words plain as day.

Carol Rose Nichols

5191 87th Street

Part Seven

Words slip away in moments of frustration. They escape in single syllables marked with exclamation points. They come out most frequently as little four-lettered devils.

One imagines those moments where they leave their job. They quit with a diatribe of chaos pouring from their lips so that those around them can finally hear the truth of how you feel.

There's the poetic notion that we will die a Hollywood death, a meaningful sentence gifted to the world. Some great revelation. Some poignant detail. Everyone believes they will offer something greater than "Rosebud" as they slide into oblivion.

For myself, I held even more tightly to such an idea because I knew my final words would bring my death, not the other way around.

Again...I get ahead of myself.

A name like Carol Rose Nichols does not inspire fear. I don't say this as some preface to insinuate that such a theory is incorrect. She did not somersault from her front door with two automatic guns firing while a contingent of skilled ninja ran out from behind her.

There are times that one such as myself begins to wonder where the natural order of life ends and the intentional punishment of hell begins. The line is faint, ever moving, and difficult to accurately discern.

Unlike my previous statement, this is a preface to the events that followed after I knocked on the front door of 5191 87th Street.

When the door opened, I was met by an older lady. The type of woman you look at and immediately assume she must be somebody's aunt. You imagine she has pictures of her nieces and nephews in her purse and is planning to make some of that potato salad that Dave loves so much for the family get together on Sunday after church.

Logic failed me, of course. What was I going to say? Would saying anything be worth the cost? I pulled the gun from where I'd had it poorly hidden, tucked into the back of my trousers. I held it with trembling fingers. The selfishness of my condition meant I couldn't even say I was sorry, which is as tragic as it is heartless, as cold as it is pointless.

I want to explain what fear is.

Fear is the feeling of a gun pressed to the back of your head threatening to shoot if you don't pull the trigger that you're pressing to the back of someone else's head.

It's being chased at high speed on the highway while you barrel down the lane going the wrong direction.

Fear is knowing that you're fucked because you're playing a losing game, and you have to start measuring victory on how much pain you can avoid in the process of losing.

I want to tell you that I'll never forget the face she made. That her words were deep and meaningful. That she said something poignant. That she made me see…something…

She just stuttered over the word "I" but never figured out what sentence she was reaching for. I finished it for her. Put a period at the end of it. It looked exactly like a bullet hole.

But that's when I heard the crash from inside like a fucking rhino had just crashed through a china shop. I heard the thunder of feet. I heard a shotgun cocking. Before I could register the sounds, I heard the gun firing.

I felt the sting, the blazing heat that met with the fury inside my own brain as I said, "Fuck!" and moved to the side of the doorway, watching as neighbors cracked open doors and peeked through venetian blinds and flower-pattern curtains.

Inside, I heard a voice that shook with sorrow while knees struck the floor beneath. I heard the crying while he said her name.

No words she could've said could have been as painful to hear as the sound of that man crying and saying her name as if his breaking heart could pull her from death.

All I saw was my window of escape, one that grew more perilous as I heard the voice inside say, "Go! Go around the back!"

I had the immediate sinking feeling that he wasn't talking to me in an attempt to hasten my escape.

I stood and ran, fearful less of the police who were likely en route than I was of the man inside and whomever he'd told to go around the back.

Passing the edge of the house I was struck with a burning pain in my side. The pain hit before the sound even registered. My peripheral told me it was a boy, couldn't have been more than fourteen.

I kept running, blood pouring warm down my side, the sound of the boy's feet racing behind me. A car came through, swerving as it almost hit me; I angled hard sending a new wave of pain through my body that felt like lightning that was only intensified as I mumbled "Shit!" to myself and again woke the angry swarm that writhed within my brain.

I heard the boy catching up as he let another bullet fly, it struck the now stopped car mere inches from landing in my back. I made a frantic move to shoot behind me, not wanting to look and make a misstep.

Cars were coming from the upcoming intersection, I could hear the sirens closing in. I felt like a wild animal on the highway, frantic. Like a squirrel that's trying to go both left and right because it doesn't understand that your car is a fucking dragon, with teeth of steel and a breath of billowing smoke.

"Eshera alth dret ereht" the grinding noise in my head said, though it at least said it without the sharp razors of pain digging into my brain.

I raised my hand and shot at one of the cars heading toward the intersection. It swerved hard, the car before it had already begun to turn. The two collided while I veered away from both. The car coming from the other direction came forward with a screech of brakes that strained to slow its momentum as it fishtailed wildly.

I heard another shot from the boy behind him and then the sound of something being hit hard.

Car doors slammed. Voices overlapped with each other. The song of confusion sung by a choir of the wounded. I stopped for only a moment, doubled over to catch my breath.

I looked back and saw as the drivers and passengers scrambled to their cars or the place where all three had met. All of them working together to separate the crushed body that was pinned between that newborn casket of metal and fiberglass.

"Leseth ekta hereh" the static said to me.

I never ran so hard in my entire life.

Part Eight

In the city that I'd lived for as long as I could remember…

No…let me back up.

I didn't remember when I'd first arrived. I had a hard time remembering when I'd left. Where had I left from? Had I ever left at all?

Time had a strange twist. It was a world where ten was followed by four and two was chiming twelve times too many.

I knew the sound that lingered longer in my mind. I knew it like I knew myself. I knew it better than I could recall my own voice. I heard it talk to me in words that I couldn't quite make out. Words that said…

"Are you listening?" he said while he tapped his finger on the table in front of me. A small cemetery of cigarette ashes that had been growing in size for quite some time had finally leaped to its ultimate demise. It looked like an old man, gray and hunched had jumped from a small white building – a world where horizontal was the new vertical.

I could have sworn I answered. I heard myself say the word "no". I heard the slushing static in my brain laugh with me when he gave me that look like when you ask someone the square root of something.

I should call him Winston. You know, because…

We laughed at that for a while. The voice said something that made me start to cough. I coughed so hard that I couldn't catch my breath. Like I was exhaling sledgehammers. My eyes watered. I could feel the strain like my skin was being pulled too tight. It made me think of when women who were old enough to know better got facelifts to look like they were young enough to make such a terrible medical mistake.

"Hey," Winston said, "try to keep it together." He put his cigarette out in a small, glass ashtray that I'd bought at...

No...it was...

That's right. That's right. You're right...

The no smoking signs that populated the exterior of the hotel were met with the Shyamalan twist ending of an ashtray in the room. And it'd been cleaned recently, so it's not like it had been overlooked. I could see if maybe I'd found it behind a bed or...

The slamming sound of Winston's hand on the table jarred me from my musings. I couldn't remember when he'd gotten there.

"This is why things get fucked up, you know?" he said with a big plume of smoke trailing after the words. It made me think of a train. An old train. Screeching down tracks of old iron. I could hear the metal tearing into itself. His eyes like the bright lights of the engine barreling through a dark tunnel.

"Just don't try to sew your mouth shut again, okay?" he said as he put out another cigarette in the ashtray. Apparently, he wasn't keen on destruction of property if it was owned by hotels.

I felt my face for signs that I'd ever done such a thing. Had I done that? When had I done that?

"You okay?" he said.

No...it wasn't he...

I was at the front door of a small house. It would have been terribly out of place in a city where buildings stacked up instead of out. Where vertical was the new horizontal.

It was salmon colored, stucco exterior. The roofing looked new. The woman had to be in her sixties if she was a day.

I just shook my head while my hand felt at the handle of the snub-nose revolver in my pocket. I took mental stock. A rare moment of clarity. Knife by my ankle. 45 auto behind my back, tucked into my pants. Small taser in my other pocket. Zippo lighter.

There's always something flammable.

"It's hot like hell in summer out there," she said.

The voice laughed more than I did.

I could feel my fingers sliding along the grip of the revolver. A cold sweat ran down my back.

"Come on in and sit down a bit," she said.

It was always easier when they just invited me in.

Her interior was the sort of thing you'd expect of a woman of such age. Oddly, she was at least eleven cats short of the number required to be an old cat lady. No dogs. Good. They can be a bother.

I sat in an old love seat while she left the room and came back with a glass of ice tea so sweet that the fucking Kool-Aid man would wince and sat down in a recliner that probably dreamed of a merciful death.

She started talking after a while. I could barely make out the words. My heart was pounding too loudly. She said something about a son. Something about a war. A husband. She was that sort of person who had a life filled with losses that had been replaced by too much time and too little company.

Part of me felt sorry for her.

I stood abruptly, but either her old age didn't let her react quickly, or she just didn't care.

Sometimes what I did was for the best.

A blessing in disguise.

A mercy.

"Bathroom's down the hall, second door on the right," she said.

It fucked up the moment like when you're about to say something clever and a nearby car honks its horn. Selfish pricks.

In the bathroom, I looked in the medicine cabinet. Took stock of the array of pills that I thought I'd find and didn't. There was so little there. Just a life slowly burning out like a candle in a room that no one goes into anymore.

I splashed cold water on my face. Stood in front of the cabinet mirror over the sink and opened and closed my mouth. I formed words that no one would ever hear. I was a man screaming the loudest silence the world had ever known.

In the living room, my hand was slick with sweat. I kept opening and closing my fingers slightly as if I'd get a better grip on the revolver. I put it to the back of her head, just far enough away that she wouldn't even feel a disturbance in her gray, frizzy hair.

My finger caressed the trigger while she started to tell me about when she'd gone to the beach the summer after her graduation. The day that she'd met the man she fell in love with.

Sometimes what I do is for the best.

Sometimes it's a blessing in disguise.

Part Nine

I'm aware of what you think because I found myself thinking it more times than you ever will. But I also don't know what you're thinking, just as much as you don't know what I was...or am.

We have moments in our lives that we find define us more than others. Like a long series of events that becomes some strange and twisted sentence that's going nowhere, but always in the same direction...until...

Monstrosity is a hard word to run from. I can look back at a lot and tell myself that – at least push had turned to shove. It's a hollow logic, but once there's pushback, it becomes a question of survival. You pull a knife and they pull a gun. Sure, you started it, but now one of you has to finish it. It's a matter of wanting not to die.

I'd stood there for what felt like an eternity.

Listening.

Just listening.

And fuck if she didn't know I was there. We get that feeling when someone is staring at us. We get that feeling that we're not alone in the room any longer. She just kept talking. I just kept waiting.

The static was not amused. A river of gravel and nails rotating in a vortex against walls of steel wool. It screeched and roared in my hesitation. It screamed at me with words I didn't understand. But like an angry man with a gun in the midst of a tirade in a foreign language...I knew what it was saying even without the skill to translate.

Her words were their own sort of bullet when I heard her say, "You might as well get on with it, son."

Reflex is sometimes stronger than self-preservation. That sudden movement to grab a falling axe with your bare hand because your brain is more afraid of dropping something than it is aware that you have fingers.

I barely heard myself say the word under the chaos inside my own head.

"What?"

I heard even less then as the static rose to a greater fury and roared so loud that my vision shook. Life was gripped in the hands of an angry titan. It was a wailing child in the hands of a cruel and drunk father who tried to make the noise stop in the worst way possible.

I didn't hear what she said to my reply but she turned back to look at me and her eyes said plenty. Eyes of resignation. Eyes that said, "I don't mind so much. I'm done here. The things I truly love are gone. You're not taking anything away from me…only from yourself."

I cried. Fuck, I cried. I couldn't hear myself under the torrent of noise while I sobbed so hard that my stomach cramped.

Monstrosity is the line you cross when you destroy what isn't even fighting back. When you grab innocence by its hair and its tearful gaze whispers, "I'm sorry," as though it was the one at fault. It's the mirror of a moment when you realize that whatever part of you was human is gone.

I was a man being chased in a high-speed pursuit, driving the wrong way on a busy highway. A man with a gun to his head, with my gun to another's head.

Humanity is when you stop the car. It's when you say, "No," and you take the bullet.

The storm inside my head began to calm. Silence filled the air. She turned around and sat there quietly. Both of us were waiting for a decision to be made.

I wanted to say something profound. Apologetic. Kind. Meaningful.

Something…

Anything…

My tears finally ceased and my stomach eased its tension. My hand still shook while my mind sped along on the highway of self-preservation, wondering how many other cars would have to swerve and wreck so I could avoid doing so myself.

Sorry is a hollow word.

Most words are.

They pale beneath the glare of our actions. The weight of our decisions. The gravity of our self-inflicted truths.

I walked away that evening like a man caught in a dream of smoke and bent mirrors. A world made of ground that wouldn't stop tilting.

The storm outside was somehow mute to me, as though my ears would not allow me the comfort of hearing heaven cry. Wouldn't register the roar of eternity as it flashed its anger and roared with thunder.

The only sound I heard was that static in my mind. Soft and cool like an early spring morning. I heard it like a gleeful humming. I heard it laugh, if only just.

I heard it whisper to me. Whisper in a tone that felt like doom with its lips pressed against my heart. I heard it whisper like a lover's dying breath…

"Monstrosity," it said.

I didn't have enough innocence left to say I'm sorry…

Part Ten

You've never had to dig a grave, have you?

No…That was a rhetorical question. I know you haven't. For what it's worth, neither have I. Not the literal kind. But we've all dug them metaphorically.

There's that point where you find yourself torn between wishing you were done and hoping you never are, because once you're done…once you're REALLY done…that's it, isn't it? It's over then. All those little whispers in the back of your mind finally stop deliberating. El Fin. Roll credits.

I'd been stuck in the efforts of digging since…I don't even remember. Like a man who mines coal trying to remember his first callous. I couldn't have told you what city I was going to or what city I'd started in. I couldn't remember faces anymore. Time was some obscure concept like gravity – I knew it was passing, but I didn't really understand it.

I'd fought the current. A man reaching for shore. A man scraping and clawing for a grip of driftwood, a vine, a rope, a hand...anything...

You can only do it for so long. You finally wear down. We all wear down. We realize that we're reaching for yesterday. We're reaching for what's not there anymore. We're reaching for God and finding Nietzsche.

And we finally let go.

Before we do – while we struggle for every breath – time is like syrup. It's the slow drip of water from icicles in a cave that's just barely warm enough for ice to melt...because for a while, at least as we see it, every second counts. Every second matters. Every second is the one before we're saved. Before we find salvation. Before someone grabs our hand and pulls us ashore.

Once the illusion dies, everything changes.

Time becomes the stream itself – rapid and violent. It shifts and moves you like a leaf in a storm – like that fucking cow in the movie Twister. All that detail washes away – it's all a big blur.

Everything but the names.

Jonathan Maravilla – 2901 Viola Drive

Joel Holmstead – 107 Rockmore Avenue – Apt. B

Margaret Fitzgerald – 23200 Sheridan Road

Darren Rouch – 6930 Magnolia

Rosalie Esposito – 4220 Hockenberry Lane

I could keep going, but you probably get the idea.

I don't know where they lived. Not really. Time was a court jester juggling my perspective. Distance felt relative. Locations seemed ephemeral. A meeting with Winston in a Sbarros, another in an old apartment building – I don't know if I was living there or not, another in an old garage that smelled like gasoline and grass clippings. There were others. There was pain – but never from him anymore.

You can't outrun tomorrow. Once you realize that your fear of death is bigger than your fear of living – that your sorrow for the things you've done is outweighed by the fear of what will happen if you don't continue…you walk forward like a man on pharmaceutical grade medication – glassy-eyed and docile.

I could tell you about the kills I remember. I could tell you about how I kept trying to piece it together, if for no other reason than to understand the how and why of it, but this isn't one of those stories about redemption and truth. This isn't the story of how I became John McClane and took down Hans Gruber.

I want to tell you how it came to an end. I want to tell you how I finished my words. How I left things.

It wasn't pretty.

It wasn't heroic.

The beginning of the end was Alice Kurtzman – 52119 Bradner Street.

I've had moments along the way where I was hesitant. I've had moments where I told myself that what I was doing was mercy for some. I've had moments that showed me the reflection in the mirror that I didn't want to see – the one that let me know that I wasn't fleeing from a madman so that I could save others from his malice – I was destroying others with his malice so that I could flee.

I've had moments when I opened doors on the elderly. Been met with the apologetic eyes of the soon-to-be-dead who were mothers and fathers. I've heard preachers in a whirlwind of profanity and a sad woman who had just been beaten senseless the night before by a drunk husband pray under her breath for forgiveness.

I've put people in the ground who were better than I ever was or ever would have been. I've fed myself lines of justification, and you've heard most of them. Hollow words, but sometimes we need to tell ourselves a lie to make the truth sweet enough to stomach.

But when you kick in the door and see the picture on the refrigerator, lettering that's not quite perfect, figures not quite drawn to scale, and the name written at the bottom is that of a child. And that name is Alice Kurtzman...

Time slows down all over again.

We're at the moment that the river meets the waterfall. We grasp and we grapple all over again. We gave up hope, but only because we didn't see the mouth of hell as it sped towards us.

I felt my stomach grow cold like I'd swallowed liquid nitrogen.

The sound of people crying was drowned out by the voice in my head. It was like a blender filled with ball bearings if one could laugh. And it just kept saying, over and over again, "Don't they look like razor blades? Don't they look majestic?"

Part Eleven

There are questions that we inevitably ask ourselves.

How far are we willing to go and for what?

Are there lines we aren't willing to cross?

Can we change?

Put the barrel of a revolver in the mouth of a hungover frat boy and maybe there's a tinge of regret. Whatever service he was going to be for...whatever it was I was working against...had to be minimal. It had to be, right?

The old lady...that was one of those moments where the line moved. One of those moments where, had you asked me those three questions above, I would have found that I had sorely misjudged myself. I was willing to go further. I was willing to cross that line. I was a coward, and that wasn't going to change.

Ms. Kurtzman was a barrage of begging. A storm of tears and snot. A scene drowned out by the serpent sound in my skull that danced to a symphony of blooming sadism.

Part of me wondered how many words I even had left. Wondered where they'd gone. Wondered how I'd look when I was the one falling to pieces while Winston pulled his proverbial trigger.

And what had I done with the words I'd been given?

They'd been doled out in four-letter increments. The sounds of profanity when things went sideways…because things always went sideways. Just enough to make me think that it was never just dumb luck – it was the game, and it was rigged.

But that was the deal. They want you to win the battle, but they make sure you can't win the war.

My hundred words – however many I'd used – was, if transcribed, something that would have looked like a dictation of an angry, teenage child playing an online shooter.

I took a moment while Ms. Kurtzman wept, her voice so clogged with sadness that she choked on her words. While the serpent sang its merry song of a downward spiral that felt too much like a needle on a record that's been playing too long.

I looked at Alice. There in her mother's arms. Composed. Quiet. Center of the fucking storm.

I threw up. Right there. Doubled over and puked my brains out while the serpent laughed and Ms. Kurtzman cried. And then I ran.

Part of me wanted to just start screaming. Burn my words. Fuck em all. Take my medicine.

I knew. I knew there'd be repercussions.

I ran down the road and let my gun fall to the pavement. I cried like a man who forgot how to do it correctly. I wanted to speak, but for all that time, words seemed elusive – held hostage to some unknown time of disuse and fear.

"I can't," I said in a voice that I didn't even recognize. "I can't...I can't..."

I kept running. When I heard the sirens I just ran faster. I don't even know why I cared. Like a man falling off a cliff and flapping his arms. I have no idea what I thought was left for me. Redemption was done. Game over.

I ducked down an alley and I heard cars squeal to a stop. I heard doors open and feet moving. I heard a gun fire and felt a spray of concrete from where the bullet hit.

I ran into the open and kept going. I saw it – a cluster of old housing with the kind of yards that look like they're on the verge of an accidental rummage sale.

"Freeze!" I heard someone yell.

I made it to the broken fence of someone's dead, white picket fence dream and felt the sting of a bullet while I tried to get over it.

"Fuck!" I said. "Fuck...fuck..."

I felt my chest growing heavy. I heard the sound of the storm in my head. I felt the world going dark and darker still.

"I don't..." I said.

That was it.

Those were my articulate last words. I didn't get to look at Winston and tell him to go fuck himself. I didn't get to stop and have some heartfelt confession with a priest. I didn't get to tell anyone that I loved them.

I never got to say I was sorry.

While the world was going dim, I saw the man approaching, gun still in hand while he said something over his radio with that little walkie they always have clipped to their chest nowadays.

I didn't hear the sound of eternity rushing forward. I didn't see a bright light. I didn't hear the roar of an engine, but I heard the impact when the car hit the officer.

I watched while the car sped away.

I watched while another man approached his body.

I didn't need to hear to know that, when he knelt down to the wreck of a body left on the pavement, he was saying, "Do you want to live?"

"So why am I telling you this?"

She's looking at me with those vacant eyes, her mouth starts to open, and I give her that look that says, "Really?"

"I'm telling you this because no one told me. I'm telling you this because you're fucked. Sure as I was. You don't win this game. You don't find a way out. You just suffer..."

I take the last drag of my cigarette and I snuff it out in her ashtray.

"...and then you die."

I let it sink in. I'm wondering how many times Winston tried to give people a head's up. I'm wondering how many times he saw the same idiots do the same shit before he realized that it all rolls downhill – direction irrelevant. I'm wondering how many it'll take before I become the same way.

"Someone once told me, and I'm going to tell you – everyone thinks it's about the big fish, but it isn't." I point to the envelope that, until a moment ago, wasn't there. "You'll be getting those from time to time. You're going to fuck up. Nothing I say is going to make that make sense. Sometimes we have to shoot ourselves in the foot a few times before we appreciate our ability to walk."

I stand and walk to the door. I stop and look back at her – that look of confusion as thick as the indifference on my own.

"By the way," I say. Then I sigh, "You know what? You'll figure it out."

COME DUE

by River Dixon

It's been nine days. I know, because I'm wearing my watch. It's a nice watch; given to me by the company to commemorate twenty-five years of dedicated service. That was, let's see, about five years ago. They had put on a small ceremony in the break-room. There was cake, of course, because those people never passed up an opportunity to have cake. There was my cake, and a partially eaten cake left over from two days prior. That one had been for secretary appreciation day. I remember being surprised that there was any left. The only explanation for uneaten cake had to be that Wilson was on vacation. That man never met a cake he didn't like, and eating cake, for him, was a serious process.

Whenever there was an occasion to partake in cake, we all knew what was coming. Wilson would be the last person to arrive. Strutting in with high authority, straight to the cake, looking down on it with a discerning 'hmmm'. Patiently he'd wait until everyone else had been served. He always insisted on cutting his own slice; acting with exact precision to carve out a perfectly uniform piece. Not surprisingly, and unabashedly, he would always help himself to an overly generous share. While the rest of us ate, he would sit there with a contemplative look on his face, clutching the warped paper plate, and cheap plastic spork, eyeballing each line and contour of the slice. After the visual inspection was complete, he'd skim the utensil along the edge of the slice, gathering up a sizable glob of frosting. Next, he'd wave the frosting-coated spork slowly under his pulsing nostrils, inhaling deeply, as if it were the cork from a vintage bottle of fine wine, before sliding it between his thick, eager lips. Closing his eyes in sugary ecstasy, he would then proceed to describe, in great detail, not only each ingredient of the frosting but the order and process of its creation. Regardless of what type of frosting it was, he would always default to telling us how it failed to measure up in comparison to the rich buttercream his grandmother was so famous for. Unfortunately for Wilson, the woman had taken the recipe to her grave, prompting him to spend the rest of his life trying to replicate her secret process.

We would feign interest and make him feel like his position as frosting connoisseur was of some value to us, but the truth was, no one cared. And Wilson wasn't just dull; he was also an obnoxious loudmouth who spent far too much time facilitating office gossip. As a rule, I try not to be judgmental of others, but he was not the type of person I would choose to associate with if given a choice. He seemed to take great pleasure in making the office a miserable place for whoever was unfortunate enough to be on the receiving end of his prying vitriol. As much as I disliked him, I will, however, give credit where credit is due; that man sure knew his cake. It's a shame he had to miss out on mine; it was delicious.

The department manager gave a short speech thanking me for my years of unfettered service to the company. I stood there, next to him, in front of everyone as he shook my hand and held up the gray box, wrapped with a shiny red ribbon. He handed it to me, and we ceremoniously turned for a photograph. As expected in such a situation, I smiled. Looking back, I wish it had been a forced, fake smile, but it wasn't. As ridiculous as the entire ritual was, at that moment, I was proud of myself. I was what's known as a company man; a lifer. I had given my blood, sweat, and tears to that place, and it was nice to be acknowledged for all my hard work.

Within a week's time, that photograph would show up pinned to the large bulletin board near the main entrance. No one ever paid any attention to that board, including me, but for the two weeks it was posted, each morning when I walked into the office, I would give it an inconspicuous glance and feel a renewed pride swell up inside of me, fueling one more day of dedicated service to the company's bottom line.

The last time I remember putting on a tie was on my daughter's wedding day. She knew how much I disliked dressing up, and she insisted it wasn't necessary, but I wasn't having any of that. I wanted to look my best on her big day. I remember standing in the dressing room, trying to remember how the hell to tie a Windsor knot. I struggled for quite some time until eventually I managed something which closely resembled a properly tied necktie. It was uncomfortable. I never cared for anything tight around my neck; I couldn't even button the top two buttons of my shirt without feeling like I was being strangled. An odd quirk, of which I have a few, including not being able to tolerate touching cotton balls or chalk, and an irrational fear of water.

Walking my little girl down the aisle was one of those moments that every father both dreams of, and dreads. It's a strange ritual, for sure; the giving away of one person to another, as if there is some transfer of ownership between two parties. It comes across as somewhat archaic in this day and age, to believe such a thing possible. No, I think I was there out of courtesy; nothing more. I don't even think anyone noticed when I ducked out of the reception early, immediately following the father/bride dance. I waited in the car until most of the attendees had left and then went back inside to help get things packed up.

The tie I took off nine days ago is not the same tie. Nor is the suit I'm wearing. It must have been purchased by someone, probably my wife, for this specific occasion. It may seem somewhat silly, considering my situation, but the first thing I did once I finally managed to pull open my eyes and mouth, was to remove the tie as quickly as I could, ripping open the collar of my shirt, the top two buttons breaking away as the threads tore loose.

My own wedding day was much less of an occasion. We were young, probably too young, but in love. Or at least in love with the idea of being in love. We didn't have much money, so it was a courthouse wedding. I don't know how it works today, but back then you went before a judge, he declared your union, you signed some papers, paid the fee, and that was it. Nice and easy. A clerk was kind enough to act as our witness since it was only my wife and me. I didn't have much in the way of family, and her father refused to have any part of it. He hated me, even more so, I think he hated the idea of us. But my drunken mother and his disapproval didn't matter. We had made up our minds to start a life together, and we would do it on our own terms. My wife—she was the most beautiful thing I had ever seen. On that day and every day since.

I can't explain the dull, soft glow that radiates in here. There's no rational explanation to justify it. No rational explanation to justify any of what's happening to me. Maybe the light is a cruel joke. But would complete darkness be any better? It's hard to say. I wish I could squirm my way out of this constricting suit jacket, but it's far too cramped in here to manage a maneuver like that. I can look down and see my feet;

the dress shoes and knee-high black socks look ridiculous without any pants. Why did they bother with the shoes and socks if they weren't going to put any pants on me?

According to my watch, it's been eleven days.

Death is a strange thing. I recognized the moment it happened. At work, sitting in my cubicle, staring at a computer screen. It was only a split second, but I was fully aware my time on this Earth had come to an end. The finality of it all was felt at that moment. There was no time to be frightened. My life didn't flash before my eyes. It really was like a light switch turning off, and then I was here. I thought at first, I had been buried alive, but I could feel the plastic bag inside me that held all my internal organs. Through my shirt, I could clumsily trace my hand along the Y-incision on my torso. There was no question about it; I was most certainly deceased.

I screamed. For how long, I don't know. Pleading and crying for some sort of explanation. Was I in hell . . . Purgatory . . . Something worse?

It was May 1963. I was walking an overgrown path in the woods on the outskirts of the small, southern Georgia town where I grew up. Walking next to me, holding my hand, was Jenny Turner. We had known one another for as long back as I could remember. Her father owned the only grocery in town where I worked two evenings a week and all day on Saturday. Jenny and I fancied ourselves a couple, but that was a secret between only her and me. My mother, among her myriad of undesirable qualities, was also a devout racist. She had tolerated Jenny and I playing together when we were small children, but now that we were older, had warned me against her ever finding Jenny and me together, in any capacity. And on the other side, Jenny's father was just as adamant that Jenny not be associating with my 'son-of-a-whore, honkey-ass', as he so eloquently put it. That's why we had to be so careful that no one found out about us. And it wasn't just our parents; it was a small town and news traveled like wildfire. Especially something that involved a piece of white trash and a colored girl. The town would have a heyday with that.

It killed my mother that I worked for Jenny's father, but we needed the money. It was the only way to pay the bills since my mother's 'entertaining' wasn't paying as well as it had in her younger days, and

God forbid if she had to put any of her drinking money towards something like food or rent.

Slipping away from prying eyes wasn't too difficult. The dense woods along the Altamaha River provided us with all the privacy we could want. There was a spot where we'd meet every Sunday after Jenny got out of church. Under a massive Laurel Oak, we would watch the hours float by with the current of the river and talk about what our lives were going to be like once we were older and had left this town far behind. We had some big dreams, that's for sure, but at our age, anything seemed possible.

My wife was the strongest, purest, most God-fearing woman I have ever known. She was a selfless leader in both the church and our community. We would volunteer together at the homeless shelter, library, the animal rescue; you name it. I enjoyed doing those things with her, it made me feel like I was giving something back, but I admit, without her motivation and example I probably wouldn't have done any of it.

Never, in all our years together, did I witness her act with ill-intent toward anyone, or anything. Our marriage was a happy one. Obviously, all couples have their issues, but my wife and I rarely disagreed, and we never fought. I can't recall a single instance where we raised our voices at one another or our daughter. I acknowledge that I'm far from perfect, but I tried my hardest to be as good of a husband and father as I could be. It was important to me that I was worthy of being with someone as truly wonderful and amazing as my wife.

She never looked down on me with judgmental eyes. She never complained and always described her life as 'blessed.' I followed suit and never complained either. I certainly didn't enjoy every minute of all those years sitting at a desk, but it was my responsibility to provide for my family. My wife took care of the household, and I was responsible for maintaining our financial security. That's just the way it was; she was raised that way, and that's how she wanted it. Thinking about it now, I wonder if she was just as bored at home as I was at the office.

While I always went along with whatever my wife wanted, there was one thing I was not able to do for her. She went to church every Wednesday and Saturday evenings, and most of the day on Sunday. She never pressed me, but I know how much she wanted me to attend with her. Truth is, the church frightened me. As much as I tried to be a good person, and I genuinely believe I was, I knew deep down that I had no business ever setting foot into a house of God.

I remember the first time I heard my daughter sing. She was fifteen and had earned a solo with the school choir. There was a general assembly held to commemorate the fast-approaching conclusion of the school year. We had all filed in, shortly after 6pm, and filled the rows of folding chairs in the gymnasium. Following several speakers, award presentations, and honor roll acknowledgments, it was time for the choral performance. I was still surprised, and a bit nervous, because my daughter had always been shy and reserved. She was even too bashful to practice her singing at home, around us. I was proud of her for taking such a massive leap out of her comfort zone.

The choir performed their first song to much applause. Before the next number, the director set up a microphone a few feet in front of the group. She returned to her piano, and my daughter stepped forward, adjusting the microphone stand to her height. The first chords from the piano rang out, and my daughter began to sing. Her voice carried through the gymnasium, and my wife sat straight, her chest puffed out with pride, and her eyes fixed on our little girl. My reaction was different; one I can't explain. Her voice was the most angelic thing I had ever heard. It penetrated me; reverberated through every fiber of my being. I sat there; trembling, my face in my hands as I wept uncontrollably. I could feel the staring eyes of those around me, but I was unable to compose myself. It was as if I was hearing my daughter's voice, her true voice, for the very first time.

After the assembly, we went to Sullivan's for ice cream. I had plain vanilla, my wife had sherbet, and my daughter had cookies and cream. I sat across from the two most important people in my life and watched, as they laughed and ate ice cream. Some of the other parents who had been at the assembly were there too; they each went out of their way to come over and compliment my daughter on her beautiful solo. I could tell she was uncomfortable with all the attention, but she took it in stride, and respectfully returned the praise with a meek smile and a polite 'thank you'. I was torn that night, more so than I had been at any other time in my life. The overwhelming degree of happiness I felt was equaled by a crushing sadness. My wife was right; we were blessed, but there was a nagging part of me that I couldn't ignore. A part of me that felt I didn't deserve such a wonderful life.

Jenny was sixteen years old that spring; I was seventeen. It was a typical Saturday at the grocery. Miss O'Hare had sent over a large order for delivery, and Jenny's father meticulously gathered and bagged each item as he checked it off the list. I was sweeping, waiting for him to finish, so I could make the delivery, and Jenny was looking over the selection of candy at the front of the store. She lifted the lid from a jar of peppermint sticks, took out two, and covertly slid them into the pocket of her skirt. Her father called out, letting her know he's well aware of what she's up to. Jenny smiled sheepishly and grabbed a third stick before closing the jar. I laughed as she defiantly strutted past me and gave her father a dismissive shrug. I could feel him glaring at me as he slammed a can of peaches down on the counter and shouted that the delivery was ready.

It was later that afternoon, after I returned from Miss O'Hare's, that Mr. Turner took me out back of the grocery and threatened to slit my 'peckerwood throat' if he ever caught me doing so much as even looking at his daughter again. He was dead serious, and I let him know I understood. It was that day, after I got off work, that Jenny and I met at our usual spot along the Altamaha and made love for the first time.

Fourteen days. How much longer will this go on? Maybe, this is it; the way it will be for eternity. Reliving your life through memories. My, God, I'm thankful for what I remember; they offer solace in this time of unknowing. I had a good life; I was indeed blessed. There are so many fond memories to look back upon. In them, I have felt the light grow these past days, and with the light, a warmth that envelopes me, instilling a sense of peace and calming.

My wife and I were both seventeen when we met. Her family had recently moved to town from Pennsylvania. Her father was overseeing the construction of a new, more efficient lumber mill just a couple of miles outside of town. There had been talk of it for months; it promised badly needed jobs and a boost to our dying little town. But each day, as

I walked the dusty streets, I couldn't help but think to myself that dying was precisely what this town needed to do.

It had been five months since Jenny's disappearance, and I was now working at the filling station for Mr. Cooper. Moments before my life would change forever, I was doing what I typically did on a sleepy afternoon: feet kicked up, chewing a licorice stick, and reading Time magazine. On the cover was President Kennedy. He was dead; shot on a sunny day in Dallas, Texas. The death of that great man really took a toll on the entire nation. Even in our far away, hole-in-the-ground town, people were in tears; they held vigil for days. Those shots rang out and penetrated the hearts of everyone who believed in the hope of a bright future. It seemed to me like the world was changing fast, whether people wanted it to or not. I guess sometimes you gotta just hold on as tight as you can and pray for the best.

It was then the garage bell rang, alerting me to a customer's arrival. I peered out the window and sitting at the pump was a slick, regal black, Buick Riviera. It was covered in road dust but was still the nicest car I had ever laid eyes on. A suited man, somewhat short with thick spectacles, had gotten out of the driver's seat. He stretched his arms above his head before removing his glasses and wiping them with a handkerchief from his back pocket. When I approached, he asked if the soda-pop machine worked. I assured him it did; matter of fact, I just stocked it this morning. He instructed me to 'fill 'er up' and gave me a pat on the shoulder as he walked by, digging in his pockets for some coins.

I watched him for a moment as he looked over the offerings of the soda machine. Then I turned toward the pump and caught the first glimpse of my future wife. There she was, leaning out of the passenger side window, calling to her father to get her a bottle of orange Nehi.

And, that was it.

At that moment, something inside me knew that I would spend the rest of my life with her. It's difficult to explain unless you've experienced something like that for yourself, but it was terrifying, yet exhilarating to know with such certainty, such clarity, that my path started right there, right then, on that day.

My poor, sweet Jenny had disappeared without a trace.

Early, one July morning, there came a pounding on our side door; the one which opened into the kitchen. I was there having breakfast while my mother still slept on the couch. An empty scotch bottle and cigarette burns told the story of yet another night of debauchery and self-destruction. I pulled back the stained curtain covering the kitchen door window and saw Mr. Turner and two other black men stepping down off the porch. Mr. Turner held a rifle in his hands.

For some reason, I was not afraid, and without hesitation opened the door and stepped out onto the porch. "Mornin' Mr. Turner. What you doin' here, like that, today?" I asked.

Mr. Turner took a step forward. "Is she in there, boy?"

"Who? My mother?"

"Don't play dumb with me, son. I'm looking for Jenny. You got her in there?"

"No, sir. I ain't seen her in a couple of days. Not sure, let's see . . . Since Saturday at the store."

Mr. Turner tightened his grip on the rifle, came forward, and put a foot up on the porch step. The other two men positioned themselves on either side of him.

"She never came home after church. She's been gone all night," Mr. Turner tried not to choke on the words. "She ain't never done nothing like that. I know there's something wrong. If you know anything, you better tell me, boy."

"I swear, Mr. Turner, I don't know nothin'."

"Mrs. Davis says she saw Jenny headed down to the river. Any idea why she'd be going down there?"

"Nah, Mr. Turner. I see her around the store, at school, but that's it. I stay clear of her, Mr. Turner, just like you said to."

He turned to the man on his right. The man cocked his head and shrugged.

"I'll help you look for her if you want," I said.

Mr. Turner lowered his rifle and left out a long sigh. "No, you just stay out of it. To tell you the truth, I was counting on finding her here, with you." He wiped the sweat from his brow. "I'm gonna go talk to the sheriff; let's go, boys."

The search lasted for only a couple of weeks before the sheriff called it off. They hadn't found a single bit of evidence to explain what had happened to Jenny; she was just gone. Over the following months, Mr. Turner had become more and more unstable. He began accusing people all over town of misdoings involving Jenny. He became fixated on Carl Peterson, a farmer from south of town who made weekly deliveries to the grocery.

One Sunday, Mr. Turner was waiting outside the church. He stood on the front lawn, gun in hand, eyes wild with the gleam of a broken mind. As the congregation filed out of the great red double doors at the front of the church, Mr. Turner, upon seeing Carl Peterson, raised the gun in the air and fired. Everyone stopped and froze at the trembling man pointing the gun in their direction.

I was making my way to the liquor store across town when I heard all the commotion coming from the church. As I approached, I quickly ducked behind a bush when I saw Mr. Turner waving a gun around, screaming at Carl Peterson and Pastor Simmons. The pastor stood between Mr. Turner and Carl, trying to de-escalate the situation. Mr. Turner was demanding that everyone was in on it, and they would all burn in hell for what they had done. Pastor Simmons stepped up to Mr. Turner, his arms out, ready to embrace the man, but Mr. Turner brought up the butt of his rifle and struck the pastor in the face, dropping him to the ground.

There was the sound of car engines roaring up behind me, then on each side, surrounding me. The sheriff and four deputies sprinted from their vehicles towards Mr. Turner. As they reached him, Mr. Turner fired off two shots before they tackled him to the ground. Both shots caught Carl Peterson; one in the chest and the other in the neck. He fell to his knees and drunkenly clutched at his throat as blood sprayed in a pulsing rhythm from between his fingers. The expression on his face, almost ridiculous; like the shocked look of a child whose fingers had suddenly been caught in the car door.

I watched as an innocent man died that day, on the front lawn of the church. A shadow from the cross atop the steeple bore down on me. I heard no angels sing, felt no tear from heaven. There was only death and the screams of the terrified congregation. Mr. Turner wept as the deputies held him pinned to the ground. I saw the crazed, yet painful look in his eyes and had to turn away when he screamed his daughter's name.

The last I heard tell, Mr. Turner had been committed to the state hospital. As the townspeople demanded justice, the sheriff said the judge had found him unfit to stand trial. When the townspeople then suggested a good old-fashioned lynching, the sheriff assured them that Mr. Turner would spend the remainder of his life drugged up and strapped to a hospital bed in a padded room. The sheriff convinced the angry people that that was a fate far worse and much more deserved than a hanging. Mr. Turner would suffer plenty for his actions that day.

Twenty-three days now. So much time to think about things. My life — like pieces of a puzzle. The memories flood my tomb; some bring with them warmth, an illuminating blanket, while others rain down like piercing blades, sharpened with regret. I tried to be a good person; I really did. But we all make mistakes. We lose our way; falter from the righteous path. When given this much time to do nothing but think, it's incredible the things we remember; the things we finally understand.

Do we create the light we find in life, or is it given to us? As with the dark; is that something that is always there, and we choose whether or not to let it in, or is it born of our own doing? Will I always be here, like this, or is there a path to something more? I've never prayed; never asked God for anything; until now. I pray, and I beg for direction, but I'm met with nothing but silence.

Is this how Mr. Turner felt? All those years trapped, without an answer. No respite from his suffering. Forsaken and left in a padded room with nothing but his thoughts, his memories, to keep him company. Haunted by the image of his lost little girl; never knowing what happened to her. Did he imagine her screams? Her begging to a silent God to reach down, take her hand, and lead her back home. I wonder, was God as vacant for him as he is for me now? I stroked my hand along the silken lining of the coffin; I guess we all end up in a padded room in the end . . .

We had found our place on the bank of the Altamaha. I kicked off my shoes, laid back, and dipped my feet in the cooling, greenish water. Jenny sat beside me; she nervously fiddled with the hem of her skirt.

"What's with you, Jenny? You're acting squirrelly today," I said.

She glanced down at me and then back out over the water. "We're gonna always be together, right?"

"Well, yeah, of course."

"And you love me? You said you loved me."

I sat up with concern when I noticed Jenny's trembling hands and quivering lips. I put my hand on her shoulder, "Of course, Jenny, yeah, I love you. I always have and always will. Promise."

"You'll always love me, no matter what?"

"Jenny, yes, I love you. Nothing can or will change that. Now, what's going on with you?"

She pulled her knees up under her chin and wrapped her arms tightly around her legs. "We gotta run away from here. Get out of this town. As soon as possible."

"Oh, Jenny, I know. I'm tired of sneaking around too. Soon — we'll get away from here soon. I just gotta save up a little more money and then we'll go far away from this place; you and me, together. There won't be no way for your father to stop us."

Jenny grabbed me by my shirt, with a wild look in her eyes, and shook me. "NO! We have to go now . . . We gotta get out of here. We can't wait. Please, you don't understand . . . We gotta go NOW!"

"Jenny, what's wrong? What's happened?" I put a hand on her cheek, but she turned away. "Jenny, please, you're scaring me. What-is-going-on??"

She continued to shake me as the top two buttons tore loose from my shirt and splashed into the water. "We're in trouble. You don't understand, we're in real trouble. We have to go. You said you love me. You said we'd always be together."

"Jenny, I know, my God. What in the hell —"

"I'm pregnant, James."

Those words hit me like a ton of bricks. Jenny looked into my eyes, and I finally understood her fear. I swallowed hard, she loosened her grip on my shirt, and I scrambled to my feet.

"It can't be; there's no way." I shook my head and backed away from Jenny. "Are you sure?"

"Yeah, I'm sure."

"Oh, my, God. This is bad. What are we gonna do?"

"We gotta run away. Like I said, we gotta get far away from here. You know what my daddy will do to you."

"I'm gonna be sick." I lurched forward, catching myself against a tree.

"James, it'll be okay. We got each other, that's all that matters. You'll take care of me; you love me."

"Christ, Jenny, I can't take care of nobody. Especially not a baby. We ain't ready for this."

"No, no, we can. We'll take your mama's car, you'll find a job, we'll get a little place; have a family. We can do this — together. It'll be just like we always talked about."

"That was gonna be someday, Jenny. Not right now. We gotta get rid of it. There's ways to get rid of it."

"What are you sayin'?"

"I can't do this. I ain't ready. I love you, Jenny, but I can't do this. I'm sorry . . . We gotta get rid of it."

Something changed in Jenny at that moment. The way she looked at me; like she didn't know me. Her face distorted with loathing and disgust. "What kind of man are you? You'd kill a little baby— our baby!" she screamed. "You ain't nothin'. You're evil! My daddy was right, you're all the same. You're all, white-devils."

"Jenny, please, just listen to me."

"No. I won't listen to this. I won't be part of no talk like this. You get away from me."

Jenny stood solid and cold, as I stepped to her, weak and shaking. "Jenny, you gotta listen to me. You ain't thinking this through. Just hear me out; I'll fix this, I'll take care of everything. We'll get across the state line, and then—"

She brought the heel of her foot down on my left knee and swung a fist at my face. I was able to block the punch but missed the second fist that slammed into my mouth.

"You said you loved me, James! You said we'd always be together. Nobody or nothin' could ever keep us apart. That's what you said. You remember that? You remember how you said you loved me?" She had me on the ground, screaming and hitting me, over and over. "You're nothin'. You're just a piece of white trash. You don't care about me. I can't believe I gave myself to you. You wanna kill our little baby. What kind of man are you? I HATE YOU!"

I struggled against the punches, tried to hold her back, but at one point, she kneed me in the groin, and I doubled up as the pain swelled through my body. She reached over, picked up a large rock, and lifted it above her head.

"I'm gonna tell my daddy what you done. You know what he'll do to you. He'll string you up and gut you like a deer. My daddy's gonna take care of you; he's gonna kill you, just like you deserve!"

I remember.

I remember being on top of Jenny; my hands around her neck, thumbs digging into her throat. Spit gurgling, bubbling from her gaping mouth. Her eyes wide and panicked with the realization of what was happening. I squeezed harder. The veins bulged, and tendons strained as the color drained from her face. I felt the cartilage crack and tear under the pressure of my thumbs.

And then she was still.

I held on to her long after the life had left her body. Her hair, her beautiful curly hair, was matted with mud and stank river water. I stood over her delicate body and looked down in disbelief at what I had done. Her bulging, bloodshot eyes stared back at me.

It wasn't possible; I couldn't have killed her. How could I have done something like that; to her, to Jenny? Her words burned through my mind: what kind of man are you?

I started gathering up all the smaller rocks I could find. I stuffed them into the pockets of her shirt, her jacket, her skirt, her socks. Then I scooped her up in my arms and carried her to a nearby train trestle. And then . . . God help me; I dumped her body over the railing and into the waiting Altamaha River. I watched her slowly sink beneath the surface as the dark waters carried her away.

The light that shone from under my feet, at the end of the coffin, began to fade. I killed Jenny. All my life, I did everything I could to try and be anything other than the monster I was. I locked her memory away; stacking smiles, kind words, and one good deed after another on top until I no longer saw a killer when I looked in the mirror. But the truth is, I was just living on borrowed time.

Beneath my legs, I felt a growing dampness. The rancid stink of rotting vegetation and carrion filled the coffin. There was water coming in, I could feel it rising under my back. As the smell intensified, the light grew dimmer.

There was something in here with me.

I felt a hand, sliding up my leg and along my thigh. It paused on my groin. "Hello, lover."

Now, two hands made their way, slowly up my torso. Jagged nails traced up and down, back and forth along the Y-incision. "Oh, James, I've waited for you for so long."

It's her. God help me, it's her ...

"Tell me how much you missed me, James. Oh, tell me how much you love me." Hands gripped my shoulders, her body slithered up on top of mine; water sloshing with her movements.

"Jenny ..."

"Did you miss me? Tell me how much you missed me."

"Jenny, I ..."

The sound of a baby's cry filled the coffin.

"Do you hear him, James? Can you hear him crying? Your little boy. Crying for his daddy."

Her face hovered above mine; rotted, putrid strips of flesh dangled from the yellowed, underlying bone. Her eyes; lifeless eyes of black, like dark pools of still water. She pressed her forehead against mine and slid a hand behind my head. Her mouth opened with a hideous laugh, and she locked her lips with mine. The baby's cries grew louder as her fingers twisted the back of my hair. I could smell, taste the sour, brackish water of the Altamaha as it filled my mouth.

"James ... You were right, James. We are gonna be together forever. All of us. A happy little family. You are gonna love me forever, just like you promised. Can you hear him crying, James? Your little boy missed you." She grabbed my hand and placed it on her belly. The crying grew louder. "You feel him, James? You feel that little boy? He's been waiting a long time to meet his daddy."

"Christ, Jenny, I'm so ... It was a mistake. I swear ... I didn't mean to—"

"Shhh," she pressed a boney finger to my lips. "You hush now, none of that matters anymore. We're together now; like we were meant to be. Tell me you love me, James. Tell me we'll always be together. Tell me, you'll never leave me."

"I love you, Jenny. And I'll never leave you."

"Your time's come due, James."

"I know it has. I understand now."

"It's finally come due. We're gonna be together, forever."

She softly, delicately rubbed the back of her hand down my cheek. The cries from my son echoed from her belly. Jenny screamed as she plunged her thumbs deep into my eye socks, blinding me to what little remained of the light. She screamed again, and the baby cried louder, her nails digging into my face, tearing away the flesh; chunk by chunk, piece by piece. Her teeth ripped, and hands tore at my throat and chest. Laughing, she kissed me deeply as water filled the coffin with gurgling screams and cries.

Jenny was right, we're going to be together.

Forever.

THE MEMORY COLLECTOR

by Robert Birkhofer

The iron badge pinned at your breast gleams in piercing rays of winter sunlight. The badge — feathered wings protruding from a five-pointed star — has become your identity. People have already started calling you the Iron Angel. Their eyes glimmer with hope and their voices change in pitch when they speak of you, their new sheriff. They say that you will be a difference-maker. They say that you will make the City a better place.

Other things are said about you too, although not as loudly. There are whispers that you are not entirely normal, that you can do unnatural things.

Your breath crystallizes before your face as you glance left and right down the crowded street. Your deputies are all in place, waiting for you to move, their heavy winter cloaks concealing body armor and assault weapons. You shiver slightly, not because of the brisk winter air, but because even in the sweltering summer months, the City is simply a cold place.

It's true, what the people say — you're not normal, and you can do some very unnatural things. And deep down, despite everything you strive for, you're afraid that your very presence in the City is making it a little colder. Closing your eyes, you repeat to yourself:

I am a good person

Though evil besets me on every side, it shall not enter my mind

I am a brave person

Because I face the darkness, others shall live in the light

A burst of youthful laughter suddenly rises above the urban bustle of the street, and you open your eyes to see a small girl running down the lane. Several other children are chasing behind her, laughing as they trip over themselves, skidding across the snow-dusted cobblestones. The girl in the lead rushes past you, filled with exuberance, her untamed mane of wiry hair flapping along behind her like a pennant. You take a few moments to memorize the girl, and you tuck the memory safely away in the deepest part of your mind.

When all the children have passed, you march across the street toward a steel-plated door on the other side. Behind that door are the headquarters of the notorious poacher, Thomas Addlestop, and his black market menagerie of exotic animal parts from around the world. The burly brute of a security guard beside the door straightens as you approach, his beady eyes flicking from your face to your badge.

"Open the door," you say, holding onto his eyes with your own.

"Just who do you think —"

As you stare into the guard's eyes, you experience a familiar sensation, like falling forward off a tall cliff. You leave the busy street behind, tumble right through the man's eyes, and land inside his mind.

The man's mind-home is a simple hut, square and squat. The front door is locked, of course, but you kick it down with little effort and step inside. You don't even know this man's name, but after only a few minutes in his mind-home, you feel as though you have known him for years. The photographs on the mantel depict his friends and family. The tiny model of a zeppelin on the nightstand indicates that he dreams of traveling away from the City (who doesn't?). The scent of cinnamon strudel lingering in the kitchen tells you the man enjoys a good pastry.

It is a strangely intimate thing, to be inside someone's mind. The human mind does not like to be intruded upon, and your mere presence within another mind stresses it and causes pain to the owner. The more that you do to disturb the mind, the greater the stress becomes.

You glance around the guard's mind-home and begin trashing the place. The framed photos get smashed against the floor and the zeppelin get chucked through the window. You pull down curtains and tip over furniture. When you think you've done enough, you pull yourself out of the man's mind, like lifting your head from a basin of water, and the physical world comes swimming back into focus.

The sentry stumbles back from you, shock written all over his features. A thin trickle of blood is seeping from his beady eyes and running down his face like grotesque tears. He swipes at his eyes and stares at you in fear and pain.

"Open the door," you repeat.

The man's meaty hand flies to his waistband holster, and you dive back through his eyes into his mind.

This time, you hold nothing back. Sweeping through the hut, you wrench drawers from their slides, smash lamps, and tear apart cushions before finally lifting yourself back to the physical world.

"OPEN THE DOOR!" you shout into the sentry's face.

The man drops to his knees, blood streaming unchecked from his eyes. He recoils pathetically from you, his broken mind forming broken words that he mutters under his breath. A shaking hand offers you a key, and you snatch it and fit it to the lock in the reinforced door.

Your deputies surround you in an instant, throwing off their cloaks and drawing weapons. Badges gleam in the sun. People in the street scream. You hurl open the door, your deputies flood over the threshold, everyone starts shouting all at once, and inevitably, the first shot rings out.

Gunfire and chaos reign inside the poachers' den. Explosions shake the walls. The hollow thunder of the poachers' shotguns is answered by the two-round hyperburst of your deputies' rifles. Bullets and slugs ricochet through the enclosed space and bury themselves in walls. Dust and debris rain down in showers. Men and women cry out in pain, anguish, and triumph.

Through the bedlam of the firefight you stride, with all the righteous fury of a vengeful winter storm. You rarely touch your sidearm in firefights, because you possess a far more potent weapon. You can choose to enter the mind of anyone who makes eye contact with you, and once you're inside a mind, you can break it as easily as you can crack your knuckles.

In what seems like no time at all, an unnerving silence falls, broken only by the occasional ceiling tile dropping belatedly to the floor. A smoky haze hangs in the air as you step over lifeless, bloodied bodies, past display cabinets filled with rhinoceros horns, sea turtle shells, and pangolin scales. Your deputies sweep the side rooms for survivors, and before long, a man in a hideously garish suit is hauled out and brought before you.

"Hello, Mr. Addlestop," you say. "Do you know who I am?"

"Iron…Angel?" he utters in disbelief.

You nod, amused by Addlestop's surprise. Most people assume the Iron Angel is a towering behemoth of a man with shoulders as broad as a doorframe, because the image fits nicely with the stories that are told about you. What people get instead is a short girl with shockingly-red hair and a rather heavy jawline. You have drab, faded, almost dead-looking eyes that contrast spectacularly with your ginger locks. You've been told that you have the eyes of an old soul, and you suppose it's probably true. After all, you've seen enough shit in twenty years to last several lengthy lifetimes.

"I'm going to need the names of your business associates," you say, looking at the poacher expectantly.

"You can't possibly think—"

You lift a hand. "Before you finish that thought, Addlestop, you should know that there is an easy way and a tedious way to do this."

Addlestop hesitates. "I don't think you understand that—"

"And you should also know," you say, cutting him off again, "that the things you have heard about me are all true."

Addlestop opens his mouth. Closes it. Opens and closes it again. His eyes dart back and forth between yours. Finally, with trembling lips, he says, "I don't know names. You must understand that the individuals who work in this business are very motivated to keep their identities secret! I don't know names—you must believe me!"

"And finally, you should know," you sigh quietly, more to yourself than to anyone else in the room, "that I take no pleasure in doing this."

Addlestop's eyes are large and frightened. You fix those eyes with your gaze, and feel the familiar falling sensation.

Upon entering Addlestop's mind, you are confused at first, because his mind-home appears to be little more than a one-room shed. After going inside the shed, however, you discover a narrow flight of stairs leading deep underground. You descend the stairs and begin to wander through the hopelessly twisted corridors of Addlestop's mind.

Passing from room to dark room, traversing damp and moldy halls, you explore the poacher's memories, observe his fears, and look upon his dreams. As you go further underground, more intimate secrets begin to present themselves.

When you have ventured quite deep into the dungeon of Addlestop's mind, you finally push on a heavy door that creaks open to reveal a dank office space. Smiling, you move to the shabby desk and pull open the drawers to find Addlestop's business records. This is what you have come for — Addlestop knows everyone who is anyone in the poaching trade — all the hunters, all the dealers, all the buyers. You rifle through the papers in the desk, committing the names of Addlestop's contacts to your memory. When you have everything you need, you turn to leave, but your attention is caught by a dingy closet in the corner of the office. Curious, you go to the closet, open it, and find it filled with stacks of cardboard boxes. Lifting down a box, you peer inside.

The box is filled with bones.

You drop the box with a surprised yelp, sending bones skittering across the floor. A tremor suddenly rocks the room, and you have to reach out to the wall for support. When the tremor has moved on, you look more closely at the bones, and discover that they are not quite human. You poke through the remains until you find a small skull. It looks like it once belonged to an elephant calf, although both its tusks are missing.

You turn again to the closet. It is narrow and deep and far larger than you initially thought. There must be hundreds of boxes in there. Maybe even thousands.

Hesitantly, you retrieve and open another box. More bones, definitely human this time. You upend the box on the office floor and stumble as the walls are rattled.

There are two ways to break a mind. The straightforward way is to simply ransack it, but the far more effective way is to use the mind against itself. A part of Addlestop's mind is haunted by the deaths he has had a hand in, both of animals and people. He keeps all his skeletons hidden in this closet, buried deep within his mind. If you expose those skeletons, remind him of those deaths, propagate whatever remorse he feels, you know you will ruin him.

Taking box after box out of the closet, you walk through the dungeon of Addlestop's mind, scattering bones at random, feeling the rooms and corridors shake. There's really no need for you to torment the man. You have what you came for, after all. But contrary to what you said earlier, despite being sickened by your own freakish abilities, a very dark part of yourself enjoys enacting your twisted forms of justice.

When you are done, the entire dungeon is shuddering violently, and great cracks have appeared in the walls. Satisfied with your work, you pull yourself out of Addlestop's mind.

The black-market warehouse is exactly the same as you left it. Dust is still settling in the aftermath of the shootout. One of your deputies, Cornelius, who had been lifting a finger to scratch his nose at the moment you entered Addlestop's mind, is just now completing the motion. Mind-time is weird like that. You can spend as long as you want inside someone's head, and all the time that will have actually passed is the blink of an eye.

Addlestop is hunched on the floor, holding his head in his hands. Blood from his eyes runs down his chin, staining his gaudy suit.

"I-I-I'm...sorry...s-so sorry."

Everyone in the room looks at Addlestop. He turns his blood-marred eyes to you.

"Can y-you h-h-help me? Please...h-help me...t-take them...all b-b-back home. Please help...m-m-make things...r-right."

The deputies are staring at Addlestop in confusion, but you think you have a pretty good idea of what the man wants. With the toe of your combat boot, you nudge Addlestop's shoulder and push him onto his back so that you can look down into his wild, rolling eyes.

"The animals can't go back home, Addlestop," you say. "They're all dead. You killed them, remember? It's too late for anyone to go home now."

You look around at your faithful band of deputies. They meet your gaze with something halfway between fear and respect.

"Did we get what we came for, Sheriff?" Cornelius ventures.

"We did," you reply, recalling the names of Addlestop's partners. "Look sharp boys and girls — we've got work yet to do today."

Later that night, in the darkness of your apartment, you stare at the ceiling above your bed and wait for sleep to take you.

The day has been productive. After clearing out Addlestop's headquarters, you took down a dealer in Palace District and raided the home of a collector in High Town. Tomorrow, you'll hit Low Town and dismantle some of the hunting bands. If all goes well, poaching operations in the City should cease to exist by the week's end.

I am a good person

The empty look of sheer madness on Addlestop's face springs unbidden to your mind out of the shadows of your room. Shivering, you turn over in bed and pull the sheets up to your chin.

Though evil besets me on every side, it shall not enter my mind

The image of Addlestop vanishes, to be replaced by that of the collector, sitting on his panda fur rug, crying like a chastised child while feebly trying to scrub the blood from his eyes.

I am a brave person

Finally, you see your deputies standing shoulder to shoulder, rifles raised, blasting the dealer's bodyguards all to hell. The bodyguards had been trying to surrender, but you had already given the deputies their orders — shoot on sight, shoot to kill, no one gets out alive. And no one did.

Because I face the darkness, others shall live in the light

Turning over again, you squeeze your eyes shut and retreat far within yourself, to the one tranquil shelter that you can always return to when all physical havens fail.

Your own mind-home is a cabin of dark, sturdy wood. Outside the windows, thick white mist swirls around your house. The mist holds terrible things — your own personal demons and nightmares. If the mist ever gets inside, it will surely destroy you. But your house is strong, and as long as you keep your doors locked, you know that you are safe.

You tread the familiar, carpeted halls to a room at the very center of your mind-home — your library. The shelves of your library are not filled with books, but with tiny glass bottles. After ensuring the library door is latched and locked behind you, you select a bottle from the top shelf, take it to the overstuffed armchair in the corner of the room, and sit down. You uncork the bottle and release the memory inside.

The memory washes over you. A small girl is running across snow-covered cobblestones. She laughs and looks over her shoulder at the children chasing her. The girl's expression is one of pure joy and of the ignorant innocence of youth.

You feed off the memory of the girl. You bask in its light and cling to its warmth. You proffer the memory before you like a candle, keeping all the shadows and mists and demons of your mind at bay, if only for one more night.

— Five years pass by —

"To our Iron Angel!"

Father's proud voice carries across the table as three glasses of rich red wine are hoisted into the air.

"To our Kalinda," Mother adds softly.

Sam says nothing, but her eyes sparkle happily at you over the top of her wine glass.

Forcing a smile, you lift your own glass to meet theirs. The table on the back patio of your parents' house is laden with roast chicken, steamed vegetables, and apple pie. The sky above you is unclouded, crickets are quietly chirping an ode to spring, and for a moment, you can almost pretend that the City is a good and wholesome place.

An open magazine rests on a patio chair, where your own face glowers back at you from beneath a featured headline. Your physical appearance is no longer a surprise to anyone, because you're plastered all over the damn media. They say you're a hero—Kalinda, the Iron Angel—but most days, you don't feel very heroic.

The media says you'll bring an end to crime in the City, but you're not so sure. You wonder if you're actually even making a difference. It's true—you have created a void in the City's underworld by incarcerating, incapacitating, and killing so many criminals. But the void is being filled by a harder, more devious breed of lawbreaker, and the seedy parts of the City are becoming even more dangerous. You've lost an increasing number of deputies over the years, and just the other day, Cornelius had one of his arms ripped off by an explosion in a crystal kitchen. He'll be fitted with a state-of-the-art prosthesis and he says he wants to return to duty, but you're not sure he'll ever be the same.

Shit, Kalinda, you think to yourself. *Just take a few deep breaths, will you?*

I am a good person

Though evil besets me on every side, it shall not enter my mind

I am a brave person

Because I face the darkness, others shall live in the light

Glancing around the table, you hope no one has noticed your disinclination to be merry, but only Sam is looking at you with thoughtful concern. You never have been able to hide anything from her. Winking at your sister, you down your wine in a single draught.

As you carry empty plates into the house after dinner, you catch sight of your reflection in a hall mirror. At just twenty-five years old, your fiery hair has already developed a gray streak. The shadows of the half-lit hallway amplify the deep crevasses around your brow and make the ever-present bags under your lifeless eyes seem even darker. People often mistake you for the older sister when you and Sam are out together, even though you are actually a few years younger. Sam's hair is sleek and dark, and her skin is smooth as polished marble. Your appearance has never bothered you, because it is what it is, and Sam is pretty enough for both of you, anyway.

After bidding goodnight to your parents, you linger with Sam on the patio, gazing up at the stars and talking about simple things. After a while, you fish a cigarillo out of your bag and light it.

As sweet smoke fills the air, Sam asks curiously, "When did you start smoking, Kal?"

"A few months ago," you respond. "The deputies all smoke to celebrate successful raids, and I figured I should join them. You know, for camaraderie and all that."

Sam is peering at the little cigar with interest, so you pass it to her. "Here. Just puff on it—don't inhale the smoke."

As Sam takes the cigarillo, she asks, "Is everything okay at your job, Kal?"

Sam is looking at you as if your answer is the most important thing in the world, and before you can help yourself, you say, "The night is getting darker, Sam, and I don't know why."

Sam takes a few uncertain draws on the cigarillo before replying.

"You can't make the City a perfect place—you know that, don't you, Kal? There will always be both light and darkness in the world, just as there will always be both light and darkness in each of us. It's the balance that makes us who we are. Without the night, I think we'd fail to appreciate the day."

You consider your sister. You may have an old soul, but Sam has far more wisdom.

"I just want to make a difference," you say, "to prove that I'm a good person."

"You don't have to prove anything to me, Kal."

Sam passes the cigarillo back with an honest and trusting smile that is somehow brighter than all the stars in the sky.

You collect the memory of Sam smiling at you, and store it away in a little glass vial in the most sacred part of your mind.

— Five years pass by —

You exhale slowly, breathing out smoke that is caught by the wind and whisked away. The City is spread out below you like a diorama, its towers and bridges resplendent in the setting sun. The City *does* have a certain beauty, but it's the same sort of fickle, deceitful beauty a rotted apple has before it's bitten into.

From the summit observation point where you sit in the dying light, you can just make out the neighboring mountain with its own city nestled at its peak. Zeppelins are ambling along between the mountaintop cities, lit up like stars falling in slow motion.

You watch the zeppelins and wonder what it would be like to just leave the City behind, to move to the other mountain and start your life over. You are weary. Weary of the City, weary of the underworld lowlifes and degenerates that you pursue, weary of life itself.

You draw from your cigarillo again and close your eyes. You put Cornelius in the ground this morning, watched as the lid of his casket disappeared under shovel-loads of fresh dirt. He had been shot in the chest during a raid. You had cradled his body on the floor that day, had felt the warmth of his blood seeping through your fingers.

You had talked with Cornelius the morning of the day he died; he always got to the station early to calibrate his prosthetic arm. He had grinned at you over a Styrofoam cup of coffee and told you he was going to his favorite sushi restaurant that night. He had told you that he was finally going to ask the waitress out on a date, the one with the short hair and tattoos he was always talking about. Of course, he had said that before, but had never quite worked up the nerve to actually do it. Funny how a man who was always the first one into a firefight was afraid of a simple thing like asking a girl to the movies. Maybe he would have actually asked her that evening, but he never got the chance, because a few hours after your conversation, Cornelius took a hollow-point right in the heart.

And that's the way life goes. For a shining, ephemeral moment, all your plans, dreams, and tomorrows seem so certain, only to be snuffed in the next moment like candles in a gale.

Slumping back against your bench, you flick the stub of your cigarillo away as the sun finally sinks below the horizon.

All you can think about is Cornelius, lying on a filthy floor with a wet hole in the body armor covering his chest. His limbs are askew, his eyes are unseeing, and his mouth is slightly agape.

He followed you there. He followed you, Kalinda. You led him to his death.

I am a good person

Though evil besets me on every side, it shall not enter my mind

I am a brave person

Because I face the darkness, others shall live in the light

The last vestiges of pink light fade from the sky, and you are left alone sitting in utter darkness. Except you're not alone. You are no longer sitting on the observation point at the top of the mountain; you are sitting at the center of a grotesque graveyard. You recognize the graveyard—it's a place you visit often in your nightmares.

Bodies are dumped on the ground around you, frozen in the throes of death. You are surrounded by every one of your deputies who has fallen in the line of duty.

I am a good person

Though evil besets me on every side, it shall not enter my mind

A rolling murmur of many voices reaches your ears, and hundreds of dark shapes appear at the edges of the graveyard.

Oh, shit! Oh shit, shit, shit, shit, shit!

From every direction, a multitude of men and women are moving unsteadily toward you, crawling around and over the bodies of your deputies. They all have blood streaming from their eyes and are mumbling nonsense to themselves. The criminals you have judged and condemned are too many to count. They are nearing you, reaching for you with groping hands.

It's all in your head, damn it! Breathe! Just breathe, Kalinda!

I am a brave person

Because I face the darkness, others shall live in the light

Light—you need light! With violently trembling hands, you jam another cigarillo between your lips and try to light it. You drop your first match. And your second. Finally, the end of the cigarillo flares up and sweet smoke fills your mouth. The tremulous light is just enough to illuminate a foot or two of ground around you, but it's enough to reassure you that you are back at the observation point. The City is lit up below you like a multifaceted jewel, its different districts shining distinctly in the night.

You switch on your porta-lantern, flooding the observation point with unnaturally bright light and cursing yourself for not turning it on sooner. Closing your eyes, you retreat deep within your mind.

Familiar walls made of dark, sturdy wood enclose you. Rows of memories rise around you, each one a shield against the demons that dwell in the mist outside. You walk the rows of shelves, admiring the little glass bottles. Just seeing them puts warmth in your breast. You select a bottle, walk to your chair, and release the memory.

The scent of wild and beautiful things surrounds you. You're walking on a trail bordered by flowers growing as tall as your waist. The fingertips of your outstretched arms brush the flowers on either side of the trail as you walk. The sun warms your upturned face, and Sam is laughing behind you.

Feeling renewed, you get up from your chair and walk to the door of the library. It is locked from the inside, just as it should be. When you unlatch the door and step into the hall, the whole cabin trembles, as if a thunderclap had sounded just above the roof. Frowning, you look at the windows, where the mist is swirling angrily outside, pressing against the walls of your mind-home.

Troubled, you retreat back into the library, lock the door, and choose another vial.

It doesn't matter how thick the mist outside gets. The fog will never be able to enter your mind-home. As long as you have your library and your memories, nothing will be able to harm you.

You begin the trek from the observation point back down to the City, lighting the way with your porta-lantern. Your hips and knees throb during the steep descent. You thought joints were supposed to start hurting during retirement, not when you've just had your thirtieth birthday. You rub your tired eyes and massage the lines on your face that already seem deeper than they were last week.

An old body for an old soul, you think. This damned City is taking its toll on you.

The Iron Angel has become a legend, even in other cities. Police captains from around the world have come to consult with you, and their officers have come to train with you. Everywhere you go, citizens thank you for the work you've done. And yet...the darkness continues to deepen.

There are whispers of an overlord rising from the shadows of the underworld, feeding on wantonness and depravity, rallying alley rats and bloodletters to her wicked side. Baroness something or other, they call her. You haven't been able to find out much about her yet—she seems to be a slippery little bastard.

But no matter. You've dealt with overlords before, would-be queens and kings of the night. This new baroness will be no different from all the rest.

— Five years pass by —

The tower of Baroness Seryss rises before your eyes, its stone walls dark, indomitable, and vile. Mopping sweat from your brow, you squint through the summer heat haze and feel a loathing such as you have never felt before in your life.

Five years ago, Baroness Seryss was little more than a rumor, a shadow on the fringes of the criminal underworld. Today, Baroness Seryss *is* the underworld. It is hard to imagine that the underworld ever existed without her. No one knows what she looks like, or what her real name is, or where she came from, but almost every crime in the City is tied directly to her.

You hate what Baroness Seryss has done to the City. You hate the army of murderers that quaver at her feet. You hate the tower where she stays locked up, commanding her minions from behind a shroud of mystery. But most of all, you hate *her*. You hate Baroness Seryss with every ounce of hatred you possess. You hate her because *she took Sam*. That filthy, obscene bitch kidnapped *your sister!*

Looking up at the tower again, you shiver, because even in the sweltering summer months, the City is a cold place, and it has never felt colder than it does today. The badge on your chest, the winged star, shines dully. You have worn that badge for fifteen years, and it has led you to this.

Tossing aside an unlit, soggy cigarillo, you squeeze your eyes shut and sink down until you're sitting on the dry, sun baked bricks of the street.

I am a good person

Though evil besets me on every side, it shall not enter my mind

I am a brave person

Because I face the darkness, others shall live in the light

Does it even matter anymore? For fifteen years you've been fighting crime, trying to make the City a better place, trying to make a difference, but what have you actually accomplished? In fifteen years, have you actually done anything?

In your library, you cower in your overstuffed armchair, clutching a glass vial tightly in your fist. These days, when you're in your mind-home, you don't even leave the library. You can't bear to see the mist outside, pressing against the windows and rattling the panes like a cruel wind. It's quite normal for the exterior walls of your cabin to be shaking — you've given up trying to brace them — but in your library, all is peaceful and calm.

You let the memory out of the bottle and see Sam smiling at you, her face illuminated by the flickering cherry end of a cigarillo. Her smile is trusting, honest, and kind. Crickets are chirping into the night. It's springtime, and Sam is smiling.

Sam is smiling.

You take a deep breath, open your eyes, and stand up. The tower looms over you, bristling with malice. Raising your hands above your head, you pace slowly toward the massive entrance gates, where a contingent of heavily-armed men is barring access. When the men spot you, they recognize you immediately and rush toward you, pointing guns and barking orders. You do not struggle or resist as they bind your hands behind your back.

You are escorted into the tower and hauled roughly up a complex series of elevators and stairways. As you are jostled past windows, you catch glimpses of the ground falling further and further away. At last, you seem to have reached the very top of the tower and are halted before a magnificent gilded door. One of your escorts raps out a complicated pattern on the door, and it is swung open from the inside.

You see a large, circular, lavishly-furnished room. You glimpse incense being burned in tall braziers as you are marched inside, and a sickly-sweet aroma washes over you.

"Kal!" Sam's voice rings out, disbelieving and frightened.

You look over to see Sam, bound similarly to you and seated on a divan. One of the guards strides up to Sam and strikes her on the cheek with the butt of his rifle. The blow rocks her head to the side and causes her to topple over. The guard seizes the front of her shirt and drags her back into a sitting position.

"Don't touch her!" you scream, straining against your bonds.

One of the men behind you forces you to your knees and places a strong hand on either of your shoulders to keep you from rising or moving.

You lock eyes with Sam, trying with one look to convey a hundred words. *I'm sorry. I love you. You don't deserve to be here. This is all my fault.*

Sam just shakes her head at you, tears in her eyes. A nasty purple blotch is already forming on the cheek where she was hit, and you see that there are other bruises already discoloring her face.

You are shaking with rage, but you need to remain calm, so you clench and unclench your fists to prevent yourself from losing control. Taking great shuddering breaths, you look around and try to assess the situation. The chamber that you are in seems to be a parlor and throne room rolled into one. Opulent décor and furniture are everywhere. Sam is seated across from you with two men standing over her, and there are about ten other guards spaced around the room. Everyone is silent, as if waiting for something to happen.

You can take all the guards, you're certain of it, even with your hands bound. It takes you less than a second to break a mind, and all you need is eye contact. You need to take out the two men standing over Sam first, but they are both turned from you. While you are contemplating how to get them to look at you, an elevator chime sounds behind you, and all the guards stiffen.

If there's an elevator that leads directly to this room, why were you taken on such a roundabout route on your way up? That must be a private elevator, inaccessible by the guards, usable only by…

Soft, purring laughter rolls across the room toward you, and you feel all the hairs on your neck raise. Footfalls move toward you as the laughter grows louder, and a woman's voice says, "So, this is the Iron Angel."

The voice is ominous and low, like the rumble of distant thunder. The footsteps grow ever nearer, the woman finally walks into your field of vision, and your jaw drops.

The woman—the *girl*—can't be older than twenty. Dark, wiry hair frames a face caked with makeup so thick, it may as well be greasepaint. Her eyes are colorless and dead, devoid of emotion. Her brightly-colored dress is gaudy, garish, and expensive-looking, just like...just like...*but no, that's impossible.*

"You know," the girl says, after considering you for a moment, "every time I hear your name, it's always half-whispered, like you're some sort of goddess. But all I see in front of me is flesh and bone."

Wetting your lips, you respond, "The same could be said of you, Baroness Seryss."

She seems to be amused by that, and her deep purple lips peel back from unnaturally white teeth in a hideous grin that doesn't quite reach to her eyes.

"Birds of a feather," Seryss says with a wink. "Peas in a pod, you and I. Very nice to meet you, Iron Angel."

Seryss offers you her hand. After a second, she frowns, apparently coming to the realization that you can't possibly shake with her because your own hands are tied behind your back. Seryss cocks her head and considers her arm, awkwardly extended in midair between the two of you, before reaching up and patting your cheek.

You shoot a glance at Sam's guards, who are both still turned away.

"I know just the thing!" Seryss says brightly, and plops herself down on the carpet beside you.

The guard's grip behind you tightens as Seryss throws an arm around you and rests her head on your shoulder.

"Just the thing, just the thing," she keeps muttering to herself. Her breath smells weirdly like bubblegum.

Next, Seryss takes a tube of lipstick from a fold of her dress — the same shade of purple that she is wearing — pops it open, and starts applying it to your mouth. She doesn't seem to care that she is smearing it not only on your lips, but all over your cheeks as well.

"There," Seryss purrs in her low voice. "Now we really are two peas in a pod, aren't we, Kalinda?"

Seryss is draped all over you. The heat of her body presses against your side and a few strands of her coarse hair trail across your neck. Jerking your head away from her, you see with a wild thrill that both of the men guarding Sam are turned toward you at last, watching with amusement as Seryss dolls you up. You don't hesitate. You dive through the eyes of one, then the other, and all hell breaks loose.

The first man stumbles backward, dropping his weapon as he raises his hands to his face. Before his rifle clatters to the floor, the second man utters a strangled yell. You smash your brow into Seryss' forehead and give a violent shrug to loosen the vice-like grip on your shoulders.

You manage to twist your head around far enough to meet the eyes of the man behind you, and an instant later, he is drawing a huge combat knife and severing your bonds, having succumbed to your subconscious suggestion that freeing you is a good idea. His eyebrows shoot upward in shock as you wrest the knife from him, make two vicious slashes across his chest, and shove him away.

The entire sequence of events has taken only a handful of seconds. The remaining sentries realize what is happening all at once, and gunfire blossoms around the room.

You careen around the tower room like a crazed pinball, sliding and crawling between pieces of furniture, taking the guards down one by one. A few bullets graze your skin, but you barely notice. You storm through minds with more terrible competence than a subliminal hurricane. You're screaming, pouring out every ounce of hatred you possess, littering the chamber with the wreckage of minds.

In no time at all, only one rifle is still firing. Rolling behind a sofa, you hear rounds thump into the upholstery behind you and see little tufts of stuffing burst into the air before the gunfire stops with a telltale click. You launch yourself to your feet and sprint toward the final guard. He's fumbling with a new magazine; he can't get it loaded. His desperate, terrified eyes flick up once to meet yours, and it's all over.

The man topples to the floor, lifeless, his mind ransacked so thoroughly that he probably only felt a brief stab of excruciating pain before dying of shock. Fresh blood flows freely from his eyes.

You turn to survey your work, lustful for more death, drunk on your own power. *Where is Baroness Seryss?* Several braziers have been knocked over in the melee, and patches of the room's lush carpeting have caught fire. The flames are spreading, slowly but surely, and the scent of smoke is already in the air.

Seemingly from far away, you hear Sam scream, "Kal!" and a second later, something heavy and soft and smelling of bubblegum bowls you over, knocking you from your feet.

Your head hits the floor, pain shoots up the back of your neck, and tiny stars explode before your eyes as the heavy, soft something lands on top of you. It's Seryss, of course, laughing with gleeful mania as she punches your face again and again. You feel your nose break, you feel teeth being knocked out, you feel your mouth filling with blood. Your head is being banged around so much that you can't make eye contact with her. You see that Seryss must have picked up the knife you dropped earlier—she's gripping it in her other hand—but she doesn't seem interested in using it on you.

Something moves in your periphery, and you turn your head enough to see Sam running across the room toward you, hands still bound behind her back. With a wild yell, she crashes into Seryss and knocks her off you.

"You stay the hell away from my sister!" Sam shouts.

"Sam, no!"

Sam and Seryss grapple briefly and awkwardly as they roll around on the floor. One of Seryss' arms swings wide in a glittering arc, and you watch her knife descend on Sam like a diving bird of prey.

"SAM!"

Sam's body jerks as the blade buries itself in the flesh of her thigh. Blood surges from the wound—way too much blood. You glimpse Sam's face, panicked but resolute, and then Seryss is rolling to face you. You finally lock onto those dead, emotionless eyes that are so like your own, and you're inside her mind…only…something isn't right.

What the hell?

The mind-home of Baroness Seryss is a massive fortress made of stone...but the fortress is in ruins. You stare at the heavy wooden doors, hanging uselessly from their hinges. A steel portcullis lies off to one side of the entryway, ripped from the doorjamb. The exterior walls are pocked and abused, and some have even caved in completely. Parapets of crumbling stone sprawl above you.

You step over the portcullis, through the doors, and into the once-grand entrance hall. Broken pottery and shattered glass crunch underfoot. Everything is dark.

In bewildered amazement, you tread through the castle. The walls are bare, the cellars and closets are empty. There is nothing to hint at the girl's aspirations or dreams, no evidence of repressed fear or doubt. Seryss' mind is empty and broken, bereft of feeling and friendship. It is desecrated and defiled.

You don't know what to do. You have never entered a mind that has been so thoroughly wrecked, and you're stunned that Seryss is able to function with this much damage to her mind-home. There is nothing left for you to break, and there is nothing you can use to turn Seryss' mind against itself.

There is nothing you can do. Uncertainly, you lift yourself back to the physical world.

Seryss is lying on the carpet between you and Sam, just where you left her. She swipes away the trickle of blood seeping from her eyes, marring her painted visage. As Seryss looks at you, an animalistic triumph spreads slowly across her face.

"Didn't find what you were expecting, Iron Angel?" she asks. "Didn't they tell you I'm just as crazy as you are?"

Behind Seryss, Sam is trying to use the knife to cut through the ropes tying her wrists. Underneath all the bruises on her face, her skin is pale and sickly. You try to crawl toward Sam, but Seryss is blocking your way, pushing herself slowly to her feet.

"Do you want to know what the only difference is between you and I, Kalinda?" Seryss asks.

You manage to stand up as well. Ignoring Seryss' question, you say instead, "Why don't you tell me your real name, *Baroness*?"

A wide, knowing grin parts Seryss' purple lips. "Do you like the name?" she asks. "It has a nice ring, doesn't it? It's almost as good as Iron Angel."

"I didn't ask for the name!" you scream. "I never wanted to be the Iron Angel! All I wanted was to make a *difference*! All I wanted was to help!"

"Oh Kalinda," Seryss breathes, and for the first time, a light is shining in those dead eyes. "You *did* make a difference. That's why I brought you here today, to show you just how much of a *difference* you made. And by the way, the only difference between you and I is that I don't lie about who I am."

You see that Sam has managed to cut her ropes and is now winding one of the thick cords around her thigh with shaking hands. You've had enough of Seryss' empty words, and you take an unsteady step toward her.

"Let me help you understand," Seryss continues. "I may not be a baroness, but Seryss *is* my birth name. I was called Seryss Addlestop once, a long time ago."

That stops you in your tracks. You have a sudden vision of a small girl with untamed wiry hair running over snow-covered cobblestones. You can still hear, as clearly as if it were yesterday, the laughter of children ringing through the winter air.

"You're the girl I saw in the street!" you gasp. "You're the poacher's daughter!"

"The poacher had a name, Kalinda. But yes, Thomas Addlestop was my dad. On the day you and I saw each other for the first time, I was five years old. That was the day my childhood ended."

You're entranced by Seryss' words. You can't seem to move. Is it really possible that the little joyful girl who you have stored in your library has turned into the monster in front of you?

"After you and your merry band of killers left my dad's office," Seryss continues, "I was the first one to go inside. There was so much blood on the floor that I slipped and fell. I was five, Kalinda! I looked at all the bodies, searching for my dad. When I finally found him, he didn't even recognize me. I asked him if he was okay, but he didn't answer. He just kept babbling to himself, saying strange things that I didn't understand."

"So, your father was a sick son of a bitch who deserved everything he got," you say, but you don't feel nearly as confident as you sound. "What's your point?"

Seryss snorts softly. "I told you, I don't lie about who I am or what I do. I grew up pretty quickly after that day, and I became obsessed with you, Kalinda. It didn't take me long to figure out that you do what you do by getting inside people's heads. I knew that we would meet again one day, and I wasn't going to let you do the same thing to me that you did to my dad, so I began to protect my mind by purging it.

"I did depraved and dreadful things," Seryss says calmly. "I pursued debauchery and violence without restraint, and I felt my mind slipping toward the abyss. It felt good, because I knew that with each part of my mind that I myself ruined, I was one step closer to being free of your control. I gathered underlings to my side so that I could pursue dissoluteness on an even larger scale, until at last, there was nothing that I feared, nothing that I loved, nothing that I held sacred. And now, Kalinda, my mind is broken and empty, and here we stand, facing each other as equals."

You can't believe it. Seryss has spent her whole life destroying her own mind simply so that you cannot exert control over her.

"Stopping me from breaking your mind isn't going to stop me from breaking your body," you say slowly. "This day still ends with you as a dead woman."

"Don't you understand yet, Kalinda?" Seryss' voice edges toward hysteria. "I no longer fear death! I have given so many lives to the reaper, that when he comes for me, I'll greet death like an old friend!

"I don't care if either one of us dies," Seryss goes on, "because I am no longer driven by revenge. Even that would be something that you could have used against me. My singular goal is to help you understand who you really are. You see, Kalinda, *I* am a product of *you*. You made me what I am today, and all the blood on my hands is on yours too. I was an innocent child before I became the collateral damage of your righteous crusade. You came into my life and changed my destiny. *That's* the difference you've made. The legacy of the Iron Angel...is *me*."

There is a roaring in your ears that is drowning out everything else. Sam is trying to say something behind you, but you can't make out her words. Seryss is peering at you expectantly, penciled brows arched above lifeless eyes, purple lips stretched wide. All you ever wanted was to make a difference, to make the City a better place, and this...this is just too much.

You close your eyes.

Paneled walls of dark wood surround you. Your overstuffed chair is standing in the corner, just as it always is. The shelves of memories are impassive and serene, just as they always are. Desperately, you search the shelves until you find the memory of five-year-old Seryss Addlestop running through the street. You seize the memory and hurl the glass bottle against the wall, where it shatters and releases a thin wisp of mist into the stillness of the library.

Rather than dissipating, the mist begins to spread.

You rush to the library door and throw it wide in an attempt to release the vapor from the room, but the halls outside your library are already filled with thick fog that comes spilling in through the doorway. You slam the door closed, but you have a terrible sinking feeling in your chest. It's already too late. You know it's too late.

Within seconds, the level of the swirling white fog rises past your knees to the lowermost row of shelves. The shelf is engulfed by mist, spiderweb cracks spread across the little glass vials, and with a terrible sound, every bottle on the shelf shatters in unison. The timbers of the room creak and groan.

No!

You run frantically back and forth through your library, watching helplessly as row after row of memories fragment and explode with the rising fog.

No!

The miasma climbs above the level of your eyes so that you can no longer see the room around you. Glass vials continue to shatter and the room continues to shudder as each shelf of memories above your head is swallowed.

Pressing your hands over your ears, you try to focus, try to regain control.

I am a good person

Though evil besets me on every side, it shall not enter my mind

I am a brave person

Because I face the darkness, others shall live in the light

But the evil has entered your mind. It has always been a part of your mind, hasn't it? You tried to pretend it was something foreign, but it has always been a part of who you are. And the darkness that you proclaim to face? You face projections of yourself. You are the darkness.

I am a good person

Though evil besets me on every side, it shall not enter my mind

But you've never been a good person, and you know it. Everything you've ever done, everything you've ever touched, is all little more than a pile of ashes and blood.

I am...I am...

With a crash, you feel one last shelf being consumed, and finally, there is nothing left of your memories. There is no warmth or light. There is nothing but...an overwhelming, overpowering sense of calm. The room has stopped shaking. You walk to the door of your library, your shoes crunching over shattered glass. Opening the door, you stride through the hallways and rooms of your mind-home, feeling the cool mist on your face. It refreshes you.

I am the demon that dwells in the mist

I am the blackness of the starless night

I am the rapacity of oblivion's maw

I am death

You pull yourself out of your own mind, back to the physical world, back to Seryss' tower. You are on your hands and knees. There is something wet stinging your eyes that makes it hard to see. You blink, and great drops of blood fall to the floor.

I am death

"So, you think you're my equal?" you say slowly to the floor. "And you think death is your old friend?" You look up. "Well, Seryss Addlestop, death has judged you, and death has found you lacking. Death does not consider you to be her equal, nor does she consider you her friend. Death considers you a swine, Seryss Addlestop, and death is not in the habit of making friends of swine."

Seryss smiles at that, actually smiles, and it reaches all the way to her eyes this time. Her face is crinkled up in mirth, and laughter bubbles up from her belly and spills out of her mouth.

You pounce from the floor, throwing an open-palm strike against Seryss' jaw that snaps her head back. You jab at her again and again, driving her backward through the burning room as flames lick the hems of your pants. Seryss' attempts to parry you are only half-hearted, and the triumphant, knowing grin never leaves her face. As you reach the edge of the chamber, you push her up against a tall window and look into her eyes one last time. True to her word, you do not glimpse even a hint of fear as you heave her through the window and send her plummeting from the top of the tower. Even after Baroness Seryss hits the ground far below, her laughter echoes in your mind.

The entire tower room is a conflagration of roaring flames and suffocating smoke. A muted pounding is coming from beyond the gilded door. Sam is lying on the carpet, unmoving.

Sam!

You rush to your sister. She is ashen-faced, wide-eyed, and trembling. The carpet around her is soaked with blood. Her eyes are locked on yours and her lips are moving, but no words are coming out.

You look around desperately, and your eyes light upon the door to Seryss' private elevator.

Shoving your arms underneath Sam, you make to pick her up, but she lays a clammy, shaking hand on your shoulder.

"Kal…"

"There's no time, Sam!"

"Kal," Sam repeats, and her voice is stronger. Her eyes hold a fierceness that you haven't seen before. "I want you to know…that you made a difference to *me*. You made the world a better place for *me*. You're my sister, Kal, and I'll always love you."

"Sam—"

But her eyelids have already fluttered closed.

In the elevator, you clutch your sister to yourself and watch her chest rise and fall almost imperceptibly. Sam's hair is matted and lank and plastered to her pale forehead above closed eyes. When the elevator stops, the doors open on a long, dim underground tunnel that seems to lead away from the tower.

"Love you too, Sam," you whisper. "C'mon, let's get out of here."

And you carry your sister into the cool, merciful darkness, leaving in your wake, as usual, nothing but ashes and blood.

COMIC DEATH

by Agyani

The window was open just enough to let in the cool air. The attic was empty save for the two people.

"How long will you continue sitting there brooding to yourself?"

"What else is there to do, Tony?"

"I don't know, get a life maybe!"

I turned to look at Tony. He lowered his head and put his hand on his forehead. The ridiculousness of his suggestion embarrassed him more than it surprised and humored me.

"You know that's not possible," I said. I moved my hand from under my chin and let my head drop. With no weight to hold it in place, my head dropped down. It was difficult to look at Tony from the position my head was in, but displaying my broken neck helped me make my point.

"Yeah, I know. My tongue gets the better of me sometimes. But you know what I mean. Being dead is not the end of the world!"

I raised my eyebrows and turned to him again. "Pray tell me what is then, Tony?!"

His bulky cheeks doubled in size as he held his breath.

"I just don't like the fact that you spend all day and night sitting here by yourself. I can understand being indoors during the day because of the burning sunlight, but try and get some fresh air during the night. It'll do you good!"

I turned swiftly towards him, which caused my head to drop to the side. Seeing Tony grimace at my haplessness only fueled my anger.

"How can it do me 'good', Tony? How can it do anyone good? We're dead! I have a broken neck, and you have a hole in your chest! If you've forgotten that fact, just unbutton your shirt! But damn you to hell don't utter such drivel again!"

Tony raised his arms in surrender. I buttoned my collar to let the weight inside it support my head. I could see that Tony wasn't finished, and I didn't want to continue holding on to my chin.

"I don't want to upset you, my friend. I just want you to get out. You've been cooped up in here ever since you died a month ago."

I was about to raise my voice but checked myself at the last moment. Getting riled up would only cause problems in handling my broken neck. I was still a long way from adjusting to my fatal handicap.

"Why should I leave this room? There's no one to bother me here, and I like the view from the window."

"Well, for starters, you're scaring the living daylight out of the people who live in this house."

"I don't do that intentionally. It's just that I hate it when they come up here to the attic. It's completely empty, Tony, so why do they keep coming here time and again when they know something is haunting it?!"

"I don't know. It is human nature, isn't it? People try overcoming their fears by facing them. But I don't want to go into that. I simply want you to get out of here for a change."

"Give me one reason why."

"There's someone who wants to hear your story, the way you died. He likes to hear stories that are…you know, different."

"You mean hilarious," I said with a frown.

"I didn't say that," said Tony, raising his arms again.

"But it's what you bloody well meant."

"Alright, fine! He likes hearing tales of people dying in the most ridiculous manners. I believe he will love to hear yours."

"Why can't you tell him?"

"Telling the story will help you get over it. I happened to be passing through the house where you died so I know your story. You've never discussed it with anyone, and I understand it must be difficult for you. But unless you talk about it, you won't be able to deal with it. Besides, he only allows the person himself to narrate the story."

"Why should I care?"

Tony repeated the motion of stopping himself from saying something and pursing his lips, doubling his cheeks in size again. He then scratched the hole on his chest. The moonlight fell gracefully on him, and the large bullet wound tried its best to peek from under his shirt. I'd only seen it completely once. It was a most singular wound. He'd killed himself with a shotgun. The hole was so neat it looked like the work of a surgeon. I'd always loved bullet holes, having given a few of them to people myself. But Tony's topped the lot. I had tried catching a glimpse of it on many occasions but had only seen it in bits.

I didn't look at the wound for long, though. I knew Tony only ever touched it when he was about to say something uncomfortable. It didn't happen often - although I'd only known him a month - but when it did, he always said something interesting.

"He's known for giving people a chance at revenge."

It became almost impossible to control the rage bursting through my body. My arms shook with seething anger when my killer's face flashed in my mind. I'd never felt such fury in all my mortal life! It was an offer I just couldn't refuse.

— — —

Tony led me to an under-construction building. I could hear voices as we made our way to the sixth floor. It looked like a group of four was playing cards. There were cheers and jeers every minute. For a second I felt like I was living my old life, my mortal life, when I would meet new team members in similar places. It had a touch of nostalgia to it.

Tony went into the first room after we reached the sixth floor. He was received with a loud cheer, which led me to believe they were probably drinking. I'd never seen a ghost drink. My interest was piqued.

I was in a better mood when Tony appeared a couple of seconds later and signaled me to follow him.

There were a lot more people in the room than I'd imagined. About a dozen were lined up against a wall, while a group of four was seated near a bonfire. Three of them were sitting on the floor while the fourth sat on a large, cushioned chair. There were two others in front of them, speaking to them in earnest. I looked for a bottle of alcohol around the bonfire but there wasn't one.

"My friend, you see, was a ballet dancer, but he looked quite off balance when he stood up on the tapered roof after gulping his tenth drink of the night. It was New Year's Eve so I hadn't felt it proper to stop him drinking. But when he stood there like that and seemed to lose his footing, I got up and moved towards him swiftly. But, you see, he was a ballet dancer, and he steadied himself and twirled just when I was about to grab his hand. The result was that I missed his hand and went crashing down. We weren't that high up, but my house had a spiked fencing running across the boundary wall. It was one of those spikes, you see, that arrested my fall."

There was a roar of 'boo!' from the three people sitting on the ground. Their boss looked at them before nodding and waving his hand, shooing the speaker away. He looked at his partner before they made their way to the exit. His exit was met with a loud cheer from the three sitting on the ground. I understood what was happening. The boss looked at Tony, smiled, and gestured for us to narrate our story next. There was some complaining from the people lined up behind me, evidently waiting for their turn. But one look from the boss silenced them. I could see that he was a man with power. I was always comfortable with people like him. They always talked to the point and listened to the other person intently.

His three minions produced another welcoming cheer when I took my place on the other side of the bonfire. But my eyes were fixed on their boss. His pot belly threatened to send his shirt buttons flying into the air whenever he inhaled. The effect was compounded since he was taking deep breaths to let the tobacco do its thing. I had only seen people smoking pipes in movies. It would usually look completely out of place in the mouth of someone missing a bunch of teeth, whose nose matched a fortune cookie in shape and size, and who wore a black top hat and a white bowling shirt which looked two sizes smaller for him. But his glowing red eyes and sinister smile allowed him to get away with his peculiar getup.

"How did you die?" he asked. I'd never heard a voice as deep as his before. He spoke slowly, giving his voice even more weight.

"I broke my neck. I don't have a neck."

"Neither do I!" he said. His minions burst into laughter and slapped their knees as their boss shook his head animatedly to show the double chin hiding his neck. Their combined merriness made me smile in turn.

"Let's have it then, your story," he said. I looked at Tony, who nodded at me, before turning back to him. I took a deep breath and put my memories in order.

"Well, where do I start?"

"You can start by telling us your name."

"Brain."

The boss widened his eyes and tapped his head with his finger a few times.

"Yeah, that thing in there. My name is Brain."

He looked at his minions incredulously, who found that even more amusing than my name. The boss looked around at everyone with a face bearing a combination of disbelief and humor.

"It's best if people don't use real names in my line of work. We used to break into rich folks' houses and rob them of everything they had. I was usually the one planning everything, so I was Brain. I always gave my partners similar names depending on their role in the operation."

More laughter ensued, although the boss only chuckled for a couple of seconds. He let his minions enjoy themselves before raising his hand and stifling their laughter.

"Now that we have got that out of our way, let's hear your story," he said.

"Is it true that you can help me get revenge?"

The boss continued looking at me for a few seconds before blinking slowly and nodding in response. I took turns looking at them all before nodding and taking another deep breath.

"It was just another day at work. I was working with a new team. Two of us were making our way from one side, while the third member was to use the other side to get in. The plot of land behind that house was empty, so we didn't have to worry about covering the back. The house belonged to a young couple. It was past two in the morning, but the two lovebirds were still going at it. Their bedroom window was open, and their amorous utterances were clearly audible to us. My partner had stopped by the window to get a better look. I had to drag him away to follow me."

The minions only chuckled this time, careful not to interrupt me.

"The third member of our team was supposed to get inside and let us in. We were waiting for him to do so when I heard a clattering sound. When I looked up, I saw a fat kid on the roof." I had to grit my teeth and clench my fists to calm myself. "He was standing there... flexing. He had a frying pan on his head, a cut-up bed sheet as a most miserable cape, and nothing on except his underpants. He paraded his flabby chest and large belly with a pride that led me to believe he was on something.

"'Stop right there! I won't allow you to break into this house and disturb the sanctity of this place!'

"The woman's ardent moaning was still audible to us even though we were a few feet away from the bedroom.

"'The sanc...tity... of the place?' said my partner, trying his best to get his sentence through his burst of laughter. I wondered what was more baffling between the fat kid and my burglar partner laughing without worrying about attracting attention.

"'I have been on a neighborhood watch for months on the lookout for pricks like you. I will not let you have your way! This is the last house you try to break into!'

"He said this quite loud, which made me worry he would give us away. So I wasted no time in equipping my pistol and shooting him. The bullet hitting the frying pan made a louder sound than the gunshot since I used a silencer. It ricocheted off his frying pan. I doubt if he had it on for that specific purpose, but it saved his life. The shock of my action, though, proved too much for him. He doubled over and fell on his back. I heard the sound of glass breaking and felt he must have landed on a glass roof or something.

"My other partner opened the door the next instant and led us in. He was surprised to see me holding my gun and smoke coming out of its nozzle, but I didn't waste time explaining it to him. I was determined to finish the job as quickly as possible. We closed the door behind us and burst through the bedroom door.

"The two of them fell out of the bed on seeing us. The woman scrambled to cover herself with the blanket as I kept my gun pointed at them. She then darted towards us, tripping over the blanket a couple of times. I couldn't understand what she wanted to do. She didn't rush at me or the one standing beside me, and she didn't run for the entrance to try and escape, for my third partner was manning that door. She ran into another room of the house. I turned to the man in disgust and cocked my gun at him.

"'The baby...she...she's gone to the baby! Please, don't shoot! We'll give you what you want!'

"I grabbed him by the neck and dragged him where the woman had gone. I was prepared to shoot them both if I found he had lied and the lady had tried to contact the authorities. But that wasn't the case. She was standing beside the crib holding her baby. I pushed her husband towards her and stood in front of them across the crib.

"'Where is —'

"'We don't have much cash in the house, but there's some jewelry in the third drawer of the second cupboard in our bedroom. You'll find its key on a hook of the other cupboard's door. Please, just don't hurt my family!' he pleaded. His voice was shaking, and his wife clutched on to his arm as tightly as she held the baby to her bosom. It was only then that the baby woke up and began crying. I frowned and motioned my partner to go collect the valuables. Our third member had joined me.

"My eyes fell on something dark on the ground, illuminated by the sombre moonlight. It was blood, and it was coming from the lady's foot. As I took a step towards her my boot landed on a piece of glass. I looked around for the source of those broken glass shards and found it when I cocked my head up.

"A pair of buttocks was blocking it, but there was a skylight. The butt belonged to the unconscious fat kid. It solved the mystery of the sound I had heard when he had fallen. He remained wedged there due to his fat. What was most revolting about the sight was that his underpants had a hole in them on the right butt cheek."

The boss snickered maliciously again, and his minions had another laugh. I exchanged glances with Tony, who scratched his bullet wound and nodded. I gulped hard and took a few deep breaths to steady myself, for I was about to touch upon the worst part.

"My partner, having not witnessed the earlier episode, was befuddled by the sight. So, too, was the couple. They continued panting but their faces now bore traces of confusion in addition to paranoia. I decided not to pay attention to the trapped fatty and waited for my partner to return with the loot. I lifted my leg and bent down to remove the broken shards of glass from my boot. However, a heavy weight fell on my bent head and pushed it hard into the crib. The fatass had fallen on me! My throat got crushed from the impact, and I've had to support my neck ever since."

I turned my collar down and shrugged as I said this. I hadn't intended to end with a bow, but my head drooped the moment I removed the supporting collar.

The three minions sitting around the fire were rolling and grasping each other as they broke into a fit of laughter. The boss stuck out his tongue and placed his huge hand on his hat as he laughed silently. His entire body bobbed, though he didn't utter a sound.

"I don't know if his thighs had gotten lubricated with sweat and allowed him to slip through, but he landed on my head and broke my neck. The fall ended my life but it brought him back to consciousness."

I could see Tony struggling to hold his laughter back as well. I didn't mind it and continued to finish the story so that I may have my shot at revenge.

"The moment he gained consciousness, the son of a bitch crapped himself. I didn't feel it spread all over my head, but I did see it the moment I left my lifeless body. It infuriated me beyond measure!" My head had continued to remain downcast, but I feel I would have lowered it even if I had my neck bones. The pain of the memory was too much to bear, and the combined laughter of everyone present in the room made it worse.

"So it is a shit story!" said the boss. It sent everyone into a fresh bout of raucous laughter. The three minions were rolling around and clutching their stomachs while beating the ground. Even the boss's laughter was audible now. I could do nothing but take my time to place the collar back into support and wait.

It took them a few minutes to catch their breaths. The boss waved his hand to signal the end of the night's session. I was the victor! The others lining up against the wall moved out and I waited for my reward. Tony placed his hand on my shoulder. I turned and nodded to him before looking back at the boss. My moment had arrived.

But the three minions suddenly grabbed hold of me. They held on to my arms and legs and rendered me motionless. Tony removed his hand and took a step back.

"Tony!!!" I screamed and tried to reach him. But the minions were leading me away from him. They took me to a different room and tied my limbs with a rope. The wall behind me felt thin and rugged. My heart beat frantically within my chest. The boss approached me slowly.

"I like collecting stories about the most comic deaths. It is a passion of mine. But I don't have such a good memory. What I do have, though, is great skill in knitting!"

He lifted his arms to his sides and the room illuminated.

There were tapestries on all the walls. They depicted the most preposterous scenes, but they all depicted deaths. It didn't take me long to understand what was about to happen, and what the surface I had felt behind me was.

The boss pulled his pipe apart. The bottom came off and revealed a long and sharp needle. It sizzled with smoke but didn't glow with fire. It had a black texture to it, almost as black as the handle of the pipe. I could see Tony from the corner of my eye, standing near the entrance to the room.

"TONY!!" I yelled desperately.

"He won't help you. He is a suicide. He cannot pass over to the other world. But if he doesn't get a certain substance every now and then, he will crumble away slowly and painfully. Tut, tut. Don't be afraid. Fear is only something your brain creates, Brain!"

He pierced my chest with his needle before removing it. A thread protruded from my wound. I could see the darkness of the needle travel slowly down the thread and reach my body.

"Congratulations, Brain! You are part of Comic Death Volume XXI!" he said.

The last time my body had gone limp, it had all happened too fast. This time, it was painfully slow. Every move of the needle gave rise to greater affliction.

The minions removed my collar and my head dropped down. I couldn't see the boss anymore, only the black needle. My entire body was turning black from its repeated action.

I'd never felt fear before. It was ironic that it should acquaint itself with me after I'd died. The last sound I heard was the malicious snickering.

WE ALL WALK THROUGH FIRE IN OUR OWN WAY

by Lou Rasmus

1.

The cat is scratching at the old couch in the corner of my bedroom. There's a little space between the underside of the thing and the floor, and she scratches at it a lot. It's all disfigured looking now. She's pulled it all apart so that there's these flappy bits of fabric hanging down to the floor and there's openings into the springs of the couch. She climbs into the openings sometimes. But right now she's scratching at the cushions again. Picking the thing apart some more. Purring to herself. Satisfied with the feeling of the ripping and the tearing.

"Stop, cat," I say.

But the cat doesn't stop. She never does. She just turns to me with those big eyes and looks at me in a way that says, "what are you going to do?"

She thinks I'm weak. And usually I am. Usually I just look at her while she goes about the ripping and the tearing. But it hasn't rained in a month and the A/C unit in my window stopped pushing out cold air last week and I'm just tired of a lot of things, so this time I stand up and lunge for her.

There's a yelp.

My face hits the frame of couch.

I reach my arms out and grab at her, but my hands close on nothing.

She's gone, up through one of the pockets she's carved out of the underside of the old couch, and I drag myself back to my feet.

2.

The coffee pot is dripping too slowly. Or it's dripping normally and I'm just agitated about that cat-in-the-couch thing. And about the heat. And the sunshine. It hasn't rained in a month.

But the pot fills anyway. The same way it always fills in the mornings. In about the same amount of time that it usually takes for it to be filled up. And when it's ready I pour myself a cup. It's 8:30 in the morning. It's sunny, and hot, and the light and heat are coming in through my window instead of cold air from my A/C unit. The other cat likes that. He lays by the window and doesn't seem to mind the heat. It makes me wonder if it reminds him of something primal. I wonder if somehow there's something in him that knows the heat of the plains where his great great great great great great great great great great great (etc.) ancestors were the original cats. *Maybe there is*, I guess, because he loves laying in this window and in this heat. Good for him.

I take my shirt off and sip at the hot coffee in my cup.

3.

My left wrist cracks when I try and do a few pushups. Each time I push up. *Crack. Crack. Crack.* It's always been like that. Or ever since I broke my wrist that one time when I was nine and I went to the skatepark with my brother and I tried to skateboard for the first time and I fell and broke my wrist into this up-and-down-looking-shape. Ever since then my wrist has cracked when I do pushups or scoop litter from the litter box or do a few other things where I have to use my wrist.

I do a few pushups and then I start breathing heavily and I feel the sweat form along my back. Down the spine mostly. And under my arms. And on my forehead, right along the line where the hair starts. I can feel sweat in my shorts, too. So I get up to my knees and then to my feet after that. I pull my shorts off and my boxers, rub my forehead with the palm of my hand, sigh, yawn, scratch myself and then walk into the shower.

4.

When I walk back into my room the one cat has climbed out from inside the couch. She's laying on the floor now. Licking herself. I walk by her and lay my towel over the top of the door. She doesn't pay any attention to me. The other cat doesn't either. He's sleeping and dreaming of those great plains.

I pull on a t-shirt and a pair of clean shorts. There's a little coffee left in my cup and it's gone cool, but I drink it anyway. Almost seems better cool in this heat. And it says on my phone that today will be ninety-five degrees. And dry. It hasn't rained in a month.

5.

The coin jar is heavy. I shake it. It's almost full. So I put it in my backpack and throw the bag by the door. Then I grab the bag of cat food from on top of the refrigerator and dump some food into the two cat bowls. I take the water dish to the sink, rinse out the old water, then fill it back up. I check the litter box, scoop out what's in there into a plastic bag, throw the bag into the trash, and then wash my hands. In the bathroom light the hairs on my face look thicker than they really are.

I brush my teeth and spit into the sink. A little red shows up. Then I rinse out the sink and wipe my face with a towel. I look again in the mirror, find a couple of hairs growing out of the lower part of my neck, pinch them between my index finger and thumb, and pull them out quick.

On my way out I slip on the sandals sitting in the shoe rack by the door, grab my sunglasses off of the table, and pick up my backpack with the coin jar in it.

6.

A girl on the bus is sitting by herself along the window. An old man with stained sweatpants is sleeping along the back row. Two women sit together, talking. Talking. I sit across from them in another empty row and set my backpack between my feet.

The girl by herself is listening to music. The old man is snoring. The two women are talking. Talking. Then the bus gets to Richard and Longfellow, I pull the line for a stop, and I get off.

The Longfellow Bar is on the corner. The Hot Dog Shop is across from that. I walk past both of them and end up at the Eazy Save grocery store. There's a coin machine in there and I empty the coins in my coin jar into the mouth of the thing. Forty-three dollars and seventeen cents.

7.

A sandwich store called Perfect Sub is in the Eazy Save. I order a #6 with spicy mustard and sit down with it at one of the little tables along the wall. From where I sit I can see most of the Eazy Save. There's a sale on toilet paper and potato chips and light beer.

I finish my sandwich and walk out

8.

On the bus there's a guy dressed in chef clothes. Black work shoes. Striped pants. Stained black chef jacket. He's sweating down his red face.

I sit down behind him and think about the girl sitting along the window on the bus that I took to get to the Eazy Save. I wonder where she was going. Then it's my stop and I get off.

On the corner of my street there is a convenience store. There's a sale on a Mexican beer and there are scratch-off tickets hanging above the register. I go to the cooler, grab a bottled iced coffee, pay for it, and walk out. I take a sip and start walking, then stop and turn back.

"Can I have a pack of Reds?" I say to the cashier.

He nods and slides the pack across the counter.

"Eleven dollars," he says.

I insert my card into the chip reader and wait.

"Card not accepted," the screen reads.

I look at the cashier.

The cashier pushes some buttons on the register, then looks at me and tells me to try it again.

I try it again.

"Card not accepted," the screen reads.

I look back at the cashier.

He presses some buttons on the register.

"Let me see the card," he says.

I hand him the card.

"Hmm," he says, flipping it over between his fingers, looking at it closely in front of his face. He punches into the register a couple of more times, hands the card back to me, and then says, "Do you have any other form of payment."

"Yeah," I say, "here." And I give him the cash that I got from the coin machine.

He takes the money, gives me some change, and then says, "Have a good day".

"Ok," I say back to him, and I walk out.

9.

At my apartment the cats meow. The one lays out on the floor, the other jumps up on the table. The A/C unit is blowing warm air around and I think they're both hot.

"I'm sorry," I say to them, "I know it's hot."

Then I go into my room and take my shirt off. I finish the coffee and throw the bottle in the trash. I sit down at my computer. There's still a tab open on the screen. I don't look for long but I still look. Then I close it and I pull my phone out of my pocket. I dial Chase. He doesn't answer. I call Reese. He picks up:

"Hey."

"Hey man, how you been?"

"I'm good."

"That's good."

There's a silence.

"What's going on, Lou?"

"Nothing, I'm just sitting around."

"You good?"

"Yeah. Yeah."

"Ok. Good. Well I'm actually at the Longfellow with Kris, so…"

"Yeah, yeah," I say, "yeah, have some lunch; I'll talk to you later, Reese."

"And you're good?"

"Yeah, I'll catchya."

And I hang up.

10.

The backpages website has fifteen pages of hooker profiles. Twenty profiles on each page. I call one with blonde hair and dark skin. Round in front and in back. She answers and she has a scratchy voice. I ask her how much for her to come to my place for an hour. She tells me that it's $200. I tell her that I'll call her back. It's 12:15 pm.

11.

I do a few more pushups and sweat again. I wipe the stuff from my forehead with the back of my arm and then put my shirt back on.

I look at the sheet of paper I've been writing on. It's mostly how I want it. Says mostly what it needs to say. Then I put it back in the red folder that I keep it in and put the folder in the drawer of my desk.

I call Hammer:

"Hey Lou."

"What's up Hammer?"

"Nothing, just watching TV."

"What're you watching?"

"The Ted Bundy documentary thing."

"Oh," I say, "yeah that guy was pretty wicked."

"Totally fucked in the head."

"Yeah, man."

"Right?"

"Right."

"You ever think you could do some shit like that?"

"Like what?"

"Rape."

"Rape?"

"And murder."

"Um…"

"Yeah, you ever think about that?"

"Rape and murder?"

"Yeah."

"No."

Hammer laughs.

"Not even to Lauren?"

"What?"

"C'mon, Lou, Lauren was a bitch."

I don't say anything.

"Lou?"

"Yeah?"

"You wouldn't rape and kill Lauren? Even if you had the chance to do it now? And no one would ever know?"

"Hammer."

"What?"

I pause and take a breath.

"I gotta go."

"Alright, Lou, I'll talk to you later."

"See ya Hammer.

12.

There's a show on Netflix that I like and I watch a couple of episodes. A bad show. I just stare at the screen and don't think about anything. But I get bored after a while and turn it off. I open YouTube, watch a couple of videos, get bored of that too and stand up from my computer. I do a couple of pushups, stop after a minute, breathe hard, run my hands over my face, scratch my back, then get up, turn the TV back on, and open Hulu. I watch a few episodes of a reality show that I like and then fall asleep.

13.

I'm knocking on her door. It's late. And for some reason the streetlights outside of her apartment complex are off. I knock a few times and then stop and wait. A light turns on somewhere in the place. I can see it through the windows along the door. And then the door opens.

"Lou?"

"Hi Lauren."

She's in a pair of little gym shorts and a baggy shirt. Her hair is big and messy on top of her head and down to her shoulders. She crosses her arms and holds her shoulders, trying to cover herself in some way.

"Lou," she says, "what are you doing here?"

"I just needed to see you."

"And I told you that you weren't welcome here anymore."

"I know," I say. I look down at my feet.

"So then why are you here?"

"I..." I start. "I don't know, I just don't feel good, Lauren."

"Lou, this is hard for me too. You know that."

"No, Lauren, I'm sick, really."

"You're going to be fine, Lou." She takes a breath. "But it's three in the morning and you cannot be here. You cannot just show up anymore."

"But Lauren..."

"No, Lou. You have to go home."

"Just give me one hug," I say. "Please."

She just stands there.

"Lauren."

She shakes her head.

"Lou, I can't keep doing this."

"I know," I say. "I know, I know. And I don't want to keep doing this, but I just needed to see you. One last time."

She doesn't say anything.

"Please Lauren."

She looks past me. She hugs her shoulders.

"Ok," she says. And she leans forward to give me a hug.

We hold each other for a little while. My face turned down into her neck. Her head against my shoulder. I can't help but cry and I feel her crying a little, too. It's a soft moment. Quiet. Late. Dark. And I don't even notice as she reaches for my pocket.

14.

I wake up feeling like I hadn't been asleep. And there's a pain in my back, just above the waistline. I run my hand over the spot where it hurts and I feel where my skin is still coming back together. Feeling where it happened. Then I stretch, yawn, and turn over to grab my phone from the table next to my bed. There's a missed call from Chase and a message from a number that I don't have saved.

The message says, "hey, this is Sameera from tinder lol."

I smile a little bit to myself and then call Chase back:

"Hey Louie," he says, "Sorry I missed your call. I was at work late last night and then went out with Rob for a drink."

"No worries, man, I was just calling to say 'hey' anyways."

"Oh, well, hey, what's up?"

"Not much. I've just been sitting around. Fucking bored."

"Yeah, man, I feel that. When do you start your new job?"

"I started the other day, but I'm off until Friday now."

"Ah, I gotchya. Well that'll be cool."

"Yeah."

There's a pause.

"How have you been doing with everything else."

"I don't know."

"You know it'll be ok, man. You know Lauren wasn't good for you."

"Yeah, I know."

"Have you talked to her since that night you went to her house?"

I stop for a second and then say, "no."

"Well that's good."

"Yeah."

"I mean, I know you really loved her, man, but it just wasn't a good relationship."

I say, "I know." I run my hand over my back again. "I know, it's just hard."

"Did you get on Tinder?"

"Yeah."

"Any matches?"

"Yeah, actually, this girl I matched with just texted me earlier. She's cute. Different. Seems like she could be cool."

"That's great, man!"

"Yeah, it will be nice to have someone new to talk to at least."

"Exactly, just get out there. Talk to people. Hangout. You'll move on before you know it."

"Thanks Chase."

"For sure," he says. "And everything else good?"

"Yeah, man."

15.

The paper is crumpled up and ugly looking. It's ripped on the right side and taped up. Words are smudged from me writing on it with sweating hands. The thing looks bad, so I decide to type it up. When I'm done I save the document to a folder on my computer labeled "Some Things," then I close the tab, put the original sheet back into the red folder where I keep it, and I shut off the computer.

16.

Sameera is a nice name, I think, looking at the message she sent me earlier. I open my pack of cigarettes and then start typing:

"Hey Sameera.. what's up?"

I can't think of anything else to say so I send that. It's not much. Oh well. I suck on my cigarette and rub the back of my neck. There's sweat coming down from my forehead and so I rub that too. It makes my palm greasy. And my shirt is sticking to my back so I pull at it, but it just sticks back when I stop. A few minutes later I put my cigarette out on my porch railing. Then Sameera texts me back:

"nothing, just watching TV"

"nice," I type back.

"yeahh lol.. are those your cats in your pictures?"

"yup haha"

"aw they're sooo cute! I wanna meet them!"

"haha I think they really want to meet you too"

"what?! lmao did they tell you that?"

"they just did"

"wow!! then I guess I really need to come over!"

17.

The next day Sameera comes over. In tight black pants. Loose top. Hair over her shoulders and a big smile between these big lips that are colored a light purple color. Shy eyes. I take her to my room to show her the cats. The one is laying on the couch. The other is on top of the dresser, licking himself.

"Aww!" She says, petting the one on the dresser. "She's so cute!"

I laugh and say, "yeah, he is."

"Oh, *he*, sorry."

"It's ok."

Then she turns to the one on the couch:

"Aw you're pretty!"

The cat looks up at her, blinks a couple of times, and then lays her head back down.

"I like them!" Sameera says.

"They're alright," I say, smiling a little bit.

She pets the one on the couch.

"Well," I say, "this is basically it." I laugh a short laugh. It's awkward.

"Cool," she says, and she sits down on the couch next to the cat.

I turn the TV on and turn off the lights.

"Sorry it's so hot in here," I say.

"It's not that bad."

"I don't know, I'm always sweating when I'm in here."

"Yeah."

"And it hasn't rained in a month."

"I know."

"Yeah."

We don't say much after that. I sit on the couch next to her, but not close. We watch a long show and we laugh at a couple of parts together. Sit in silence during the slow parts. And then the show is over.

I look at her and ask if she wants to watch another episode.

She yawns and says, "not really. I think I might head home."

"Oh, ok."

"Yeah, I actually have to work later."

I sit up from the couch and turn the lights back on.

"Gotchya."

But she just sits there petting the cat for a second. She taps her knee with her free hand. Then she gets up and walks over to me. I don't say anything. I just stand there and look down at her. She stands there and looks back at me. Her big eyes looking back at me. And I can't help but lean in.

"Hey," she says, backing away.

I lean back and say that I'm sorry.

"No," she says, and then she jumps up into me. She kisses me hard with those big lips and I kiss her hard right back, wrapping my arms around her and pulling her into me.

"Ok, ok," she says. She steps back. "That's it for now. I have to go."

I run my hand over my face. Her lipstick rubs off on my hand.

"Sorry," she says. "Here." And she reaches up and wipes lipstick off of my chin.

"Thanks," I say, laughing a little bit.

"Ok, I have to go though."

"Ok."

18.

There are still messages from Lauren on my phone. I lay in bed and look through them:

"I'm so sorry Lauren"

"FUCK YOU LOU!"

"Lauren I love you. I was drunk. It was a mistake!"

"YOU ARE DISGUSTING!"

"I know I know"

"NO YOU MAKE ME SICK!"

I stop reading after that. I know where the conversation goes. Then I hang my finger over the trash can symbol on my phone, telling myself to delete the messages. But I don't.

19.

Hammer texts me and asks me if I want to get drunk. I look at the message and then put my phone down. The cat meows at me. She has a rubber band at her feet. A cat that likes to fetch. She's funny like that. So I grab the rubber band and shoot it out of my room. She goes leaping after it. The other cat just lays on my dresser and watches. He has a funny look on his face watching her. And then she brings it back, drops it at her feet, and waits for me to fling the thing again. I do. She brings it back. And it goes on like that for a little while. It goes on until she's worn herself out and she's ready to lay back down and lick herself some more. When she's done playing I go back outside for another cigarette. It's getting late and the sun has gone down. There are a few bugs swarming the light on my back porch. I text Sameera and tell her that it was nice meeting her and hanging out. A few minutes later she texts me back and says that she had fun, too.

20.

In the morning I get up and make coffee. I throw some laundry in the wash and I empty the litter box. I load a couple of dirty dishes into the dishwasher and start it. I straighten the pillows and the blanket on my bed. I clip my fingernails and toenails. I smack the A/C unit and curse it, swearing to burn it into nothing if it doesn't start pushing out cold air. The app on my phone says that the high today is ninety-seven degrees. And dry. I do a few pushups but give up after a couple of minutes. The dream I had during the night is still playing in my head:

Lauren has my wine key in her hand. She grabbed it from my back pocket. We were hugging. I wasn't paying attention. And now she has the corkscrew pointing at me.

"Lauren."

She takes a step back and holds the thing in front of me.

"Lauren."

"You need to leave, Lou!"

I put my hands up. Palms open.

"Lauren!"

"NOW!"

"Please," I say softly. "Please."

And she lowers the point of the screw. I can see her shaking.

"Lauren, I'm sorry."

She doesn't move.

"I'm so, so sorry. I never meant to do this. I never wanted to do this. I fucked up. I know. I fucked it all up. And it sucks, because what we had was so beautiful... it could've been so beautiful... it could still be so beautiful Lauren! Just let me try again! I'll show you I can be better!"

She starts shaking her head. There's water in her eyes and they're all swollen looking.

"Lauren," I say. "It can all be better. I was drunk. It was nothing. I never meant any of it."

"That's just an excuse."

"Yes, it is. But I can't say anything that will change it. I can't say anything that will make it all go away. But I can promise that things will change. I can promise..."

"I don't want your promises, Lou."

I stop. I don't say anything. I don't move.

She stands there. Shaking more.

"Lou," she says. "I need you to leave."

"Lauren please..."

"No. Lou, I can't have you in my life anymore. I can't have us in my life anymore. I need to take care of myself. Physically. Mentally. And emotionally. I need this to be over."

There's a hard spot in my throat.

"Lou," she says. "Please go."

And I don't say anything back. I look down at my feet.

"Please."

I look back up at her.

"Lauren."

She shakes her head.

"Can I just have one more hug?"

She stands and looks back at me.

"Just one last time," I say.

There's a creak in the floor as she shifts her weight from one side to the other. Her dog barks from somewhere back in the house.

"Bully!" She yells out. "Quiet!"

"Aw."

Lauren looks back to me.

"How is he?" I ask.

"He's fine."

"Good."

"Yeah."

And then we both stand there looking at each other.

"Lauren, can I please just have a hug?"

She doesn't move.

"Please."

And she opens her arms. She starts crying and she wraps around me the same way she wrapped around me before. She's still shaking but she feels warm against me. I bring her into me tight.

It takes a few seconds for me to remember that she was still holding the corkscrew.

21.

The laundry is done. I hear the dryer shut off. So I get up and take the clothes out and fold them and put them away. The dishes in the dishwasher are clean so I take them out and put them back into the cabinets. The one cat meows at me when I take the plates from the bottom rack. I tell him to shut up. He meows anyway. His bowl is empty.

"Shit, I'm sorry," I tell him.

"Meow."

"Yeah, yeah I got it."

"Meow."

I fill his bowl and tell him to shut up again.

"Meow."

"Ok, eat."

And he does. Then the other cat comes up between my feet and so I fill her bowl too. She eats along with the other one.

"Enjoy," I say to them. Then I take the vacuum out of the closet and vacuum the rug in my living room. It doesn't work very well. Cat hair is stuck deep into the thing. But I vacuum it for a little bit anyway because it keeps me busy for a few minutes.

I text Sameera after that.

She texts back and says, "hi."

"I'm free," I type back.

"me too."

"want to come over"

"u come here"

"ok," I text her, and then I go to her place.

22.

Sameera lives on the east side of the city. Nice place. Big and old like most of the other apartment buildings on the east side of the city. She lets me inside and shows me around. There's not much in the place. A white couch and a little TV on a black TV stand across from the couch. Glass table in between the two. Thick, purple rug underneath. None of it really goes together.

Her room is off of the living room and she shows me that too. She has a big bed that she keeps on the floor and a dresser from IKEA. Bookshelf across from the dresser. She has a couple of things by one of the authors that I like and I ask her about him.

"Yeah, I love his poetry."

"Really?"

"Yeah, I've read most of his stuff. You know him?"

"Yeah," I say. "But I like his novels a little more than the poetry."

"Cool."

She shows me through the kitchen after that and then out onto the back porch. She has a little yard behind that and she tells me that she loves having the yard. She says that it reminds her of being back at her parent's house. I tell her that I like the yard too.

"Do you want a cigarette?" she asks me.

I pull out my own pack.

She laughs and says, "ok then."

I laugh with her and then we both light our cigarettes. We stand in silence for a little while, just dragging and exhaling and listening to the music playing from some balcony a few buildings down. A few of the songs are good.

"I know these guys," she says.

"What?"

"This song. Can you hear it?"

"Yeah, I feel like I know it."

"It's Cherish, by The Lost Spirits."

"Ok yeah, I've heard of them. You know them?"

"Yeah. They're from my hometown. The bassist's brother was in my grade. They moved to the city a few years ago and they play a lot around here. I've seen them a few times."

I look up their profile on my phone.

"They're top song has millions of plays."

She pulls on her cigarette and then says, "yeah."

"That's cool."

"Yeah."

I put my cigarette out.

"Do you want to watch a movie?"

"Sure."

23.

When she puts her clothes back on the movie is still playing. She reaches for her cigarettes and asks if I want to have one.

I pull my shirt on and say, "Sure."

She slips her feet into her shoes and she puts on a sweatshirt.

I look down at the bed and then up at her.

"Sorry about all that."

"It's ok," she says, "I can wash the sheets."

"Ok."

And we go back outside. The music from earlier isn't playing anymore but the sound of traffic is soft in the distance. It's getting late but there are still cars going past the front of the place. The bars must still be open.

"It hasn't rained in a while," I say.

"I know," she says. "You told me the other day."

"I wish it would just rain."

"I guess."

I pull on my cigarette. She pulls on hers. And then I tell her that I'm going to go home.

"Ok," she says.

"Do you want to hang out again sometime?"

"Sure."

24.

There's not much left to write on this page. I have the document open on my computer again and, looking at it, I decide that it says everything that I need it to say, so I open my email, and I upload it to a draft message. Then I close my computer.

My phone starts buzzing. It's Chase:

"Hey," I say.

"Louieeee, how are you?"

I laugh a little and tell him that I'm fine. He asks me how things are going. I tell him that things are about the same. Or maybe a little better now. I tell him that the new girl from Tinder is a good distraction, even if it hasn't been very exciting, and I tell him that I'm ready to get back to my new job tomorrow. He says that that all sounds good. He says that it's good to rebound, and that the job will be good for me.

"Yeah," I say, "it will be."

Then we talk about a couple of other little things before we both hang up.

25.

The cat jumps on my lap when I put my phone down. She purrs and rubs her face against my chest and then she lays down across my knees. I scratch her head and pet her down her back. The other cat jumps up on my dresser and looks at us. He blinks a couple of times before he lays his head down and falls asleep. I turn on Netflix and watch a couple of shows. The cat jumps off of me after a while and so I get in bed. The place is still hot so I lay on top of the comforter. I want to sleep but nothing happens. My eyes won't close. And so I just lay there, watching episodes of another bad show, trying not to think about anything but thinking about things anyway. Until my phone lights up. I left it on the desk, but I can see it light up. And it buzzes. It buzzes a few times. I don't want to get up but when the lights and the buzzing go off for the seventh time I pull myself from the mattress and crawl to the desk. The messages are all from Reese:

"Lou," the first one reads, "cmon man answer your phone"

I look through the notifications bar. I have three missed calls too.

The next few messages say, "im sorry I couldnt talk earlier… Kris doesnt like it when im on my phone when we're together… but she just went home so call me back"

I text him back and tell him that I'm tired. I tell him I don't really want to talk.

He calls me the next minute:

"Lou," he says.

"Yeah?"

"How are you?"

"I'm good. How was The Longfellow?"

"Good. You haven't been by in a while."

"Yeah."

"Like a month or so?"

"Yeah."

He takes a heavy breath.

"So what's wrong Lou? Is this about Lauren?"

"I don't know."

"What do you mean?"

"Maybe it is."

"When was the last time you saw her?"

A raindrop hits my window. I watch it splatter and then roll down the glass. Another drop hits after that. And another. And then it stops.

"Lou?"

"Yeah," I say, "yeah. Sorry. No, I haven't seen her in the last couple of weeks."

The image flashes in my mind. The last time I saw Lauren. I see it like I've seen it in the dreams that I keep having:

She's falling backwards. I push her off of me and she starts falling backwards. I've never even pointed a finger in her face before. Hardly raised my voice. But now she's falling backwards off of me. The corkscrew is in my back, just above the waistline. She screams. That's the last thing that happens. She screams and the back of her head cracks against the radiator. The sound of it wakes up Bully and the dog comes running out into the room. There's blood pooling around Lauren. The dog licks her face and barks and nudges her shoulder with his nose. He doesn't understand. And I don't understand. And I can't really focus on any of it because of the pain in my back. Pain down through my legs and up through my spine. Everything is burning. I reach for the handle of the thing but touching it sends this splitting feeling through my body so I leave it where it is. There's a ringing between my ears and my vision is blurry. The room is spinning and my feet aren't working well. I feel like I'm going to vomit, but I stumble over to Lauren anyway. Bully is still trying to wake her up so I push him away. He barks at me. I tell him to be quiet. He still doesn't understand.

"Okay, Lauren," I say, and I start dragging her across the living room. She's such a small girl. Fragile. But she feels heavy right now. Or there's too much friction with the carpet. There's red pouring into the fabric and trailing behind her as I get her to the bathroom. And I don't know what to do about her head but I think putting her in the tub is a good idea. I want to give her a bath. She likes baths. She always says that baths help her relax. So I put her in the tub and take her clothes off. She looks good so I tell her that she looks good but she doesn't say anything back. She's bleeding more now. I am too. But she looks good so I lean into the tub and I give her a kiss. I wrap my arms around her and pull her towards me. She doesn't wrap her arms around me but she still feels good against me so I hold her tight. I kiss her neck and I taste the red on my lips. I feel it running over my arms too. And it's running from me too, down my legs.

"I guess I should take a bath, too," I say to the walls.

Bully looks up at me with his head turned to the side.

Then I start getting undressed. I can't take my shirt off because of the pain but I get my shoes and my pants off and then I roll into the tub with her. I run the water and it's cold at first but after a little while it's warm and together we're warm and for just a little bit in that moment the pain goes away.

"Lou!"

My eyes come back to the window in my room.

"Lou," Reese says again, "can you hear me?"

"Yeah," I say.

"I asked if you wanted to come to The Longfellow tomorrow. It's wing night. Hammer said he's coming."

I blink and blink and I rub my face with my hand.

"I can't," I say.

"Why not?"

"I have work tomorrow."

"Work where."

"A new restaurant. I just started the other day."

"Man. Alright. Well next time, you should come."

"Yeah."

"And you're good? Like about Lauren and everything."

"Yeah, Reese. Thanks."

26.

I open the draft on my computer and type in Lauren's parents email. I don't type much of a message. It just says the "Dear Mr. & Mrs." part and the "I'm sorry" part and the "it's all explained in the attached document" part. And the attached document explains it all. It explains how Lauren is still in the tub. It says how I left her there. And it says that I took the dog with me, walked him down the street and into the little walking path where Lauren would walk him, and held him down until he stopped whimpering and fighting back. It says how I'm sorry about that but that I didn't know what else to do. And it says that I took Lauren's phone with me so I could respond to anyone who messaged or called. It tells them that I'm sorry for making it sound like

Lauren didn't want to see them last weekend. And then it says that it's not about me, but that I tried to kill myself but I got scared and I couldn't do it. It says that I will turn myself in after I send this email. It says everything I need it to say, so I put my name at the bottom of the message and press 'send.'

27.

The next day Sameera asks me if I want to come over again. My shift is at noon but I don't tell her that. I don't plan on showing up anyway. So I tell her that I'll come over. I tell her that I really want to see her again. Then I make some coffee fill the cat bowls fix my bed empty the litter box drink my coffee brush my teeth call the police and tell them everything about that night give them Sameera's address and leave for her apartment.

"Meow," the one cat says.

"Yeah, yeah," I say back. "I'll catchya."

Then I shut the door.

28.

The 67 bus is full. A few old women in the first row are talking in Spanish about something and a couple of young women in the fourth row are talking about their boyfriends. There are two men dressed like carpenters or electricians or something blue collar along the back row. An old couple is holding hands in the handicap seats. A few kids with skateboards stand in the aisle by the door. I grab the rail along the ceiling of the thing and sweat on myself as the bus pulls away from the curb.

After a few miles I get off. The 15 bus starts at the corner of Richard and Longfellow and then runs the rest of the way into the east side of the city so I go over to the stop and wait for it. The Hot Dog Shop is right there so I step in and get a hot dog and fries. The Longfellow is across the street and I see Reese's car in the lot.

"Nine dollars," the guy at the counter says.

I hand him my card.

"Cash only."

"Ok," I say, and I put my card back.

The guy looks down at me. His fat cheeks look heavy and tired from hanging onto his face in this heat.

"I only have seven dollars," I say.

He points to the end of the counter.

"There's the ATM."

"Ok."

And I go to the ATM. I take out twenty dollars. Then I go back to him at the counter, give him twenty dollars, take the eleven dollars back for my change, leave him a dollar, and take my hot dog and fries and walk out.

The 15 bus pulls up but it's full and I'm still eating and so I let it go. The hot dog isn't anything great but the fries are salted with the right amount of salt so I enjoy them for the most part. When I'm done, I'm sweating bad. The app on my phone says that today will be ninety-six and dry.

THE CANCEROUS AFFAIR

by Braeden Michaels

JASON

"What are you going to do? Seriously. Are you going to give me less sex? You already *do* that!"

"What the fuck did you just say?"

"You heard me. You are a lazy lover. It's like pulling teeth."

I walked around aggravated to the core and grabbed the suitcase from the closet. She stood there, looking astonished.

"Jason, what are you doing?" She looked incredulous.

"What does it look like I'm doing? I'm packing some clothes and heading to my brother's house. I will come back later to get the rest of my things."

"You are going to throw away a marriage of ten years over a sandwich you ate? Yeah, I was upset but damn Jason, this is ridiculous."

"You know it's about more than just a damn sandwich."

I got tired of looking at her and went back to packing. I refused to look at her.

"So our marriage is going to end because we don't have sex as much as you like?"

I threw the suitcase down with disgust.

"Look at me Melissa. Take a real close look. I am so tired of defending myself and explaining what I need. I'm not saying you are a bitch or a bad person, but you just don't give me what I want in a relationship. I have to remind you what I want every few months. You do it for a week or two then you don't put any effort into us. That's the real problem here. It's not just about sex. It's so much more. I am a writer at heart and I never get the chance to do what I want to do."

A part of me didn't care about the tears forming in her eyes. I started to walk past her.

"Stop. I love you Jason. You are my world and I need you."

I walked into the kitchen and opened up the refrigerator in silence. I grabbed a Sam Adams and sat down on the couch. Melissa was sobbing in front of me.

"I want you to think about what you just said." I growled out. "I don't want to be a need. I don't want to be a tool you use once in a while. I don't want to be a requirement or an obligation. I want you to show interest in what I do because you want to. I want you to do stuff sexually because you want to do it. It comes across that you do the bare minimum just to keep me here. There were things you did in the beginning of our relationship but somewhere along the way, you just...stopped."

Her sobbing slowed, stopped. "Jason do you remember when it all changed?"

"Yes, I do."

"When? Tell me, when."

"After Mark's funeral."

"What happened the day of the funeral?"

I took a swig of beer and closed my eyes for a second. I tried so hard to forget that day. *I could hear my cell phone ringing in the pitch dark over and over. I could feel her lips and tongue masterfully sucking my cock as we stood in the bathroom. There was no room in there. My ass was painfully rubbing against the sink as she engulfed me. I came within seconds. Jen stood up and kissed my lips.*

"I will text you when you can come out. I need to go to talk to the pastor."

I stood in the dark and saw my phone go off again.

"Where are you?"

"I'm in the bathroom. I will be out in a few minutes."

"You have been gone quite a while and the pastor has been looking for Jen."

"Maybe she's in the bathroom."

Melissa hung up. I stood there waiting for Jen's text. I kept on thinking about Mark and our friendship over the years.

Shortly her text came that I could leave the bathroom.

There wasn't a dry eye in the funeral hall. I sat next to Melissa and held her hand throughout the session.

The eulogy reverberated in my ears as tears fell endlessly around me. I could hear her voice struggle with composure. The edges of my soul burnt to a crisp. I could hear her say over and over how much she loved Mark. They were supposed to have a lifetime together and God took him away at the age of forty. Suddenly, I couldn't wait for this to end. She looked like a mess as she spoke. We all said our goodbyes to Mark. It was the hardest thing I had to do. I couldn't believe I was seeing him in a casket.

"Look at me, Jason. Come on. LOOK AT ME!"

"Yes, I remember that day. It's coming back to me."

"Do you remember when we all went back to her house?"

I took another swig of beer and closed my eyes again.

"Jen, you should stop drinking. People are noticing; you're slurring your words. Please stop."

"You don't tell me what the fuck to do. Is your husband dead?"

"No, but my best friend is dead. I am hurting too, just like you."

"Are you really hurting? He has had cancer for four years and you have fucked every hole of me in all of that time. You had no problem doing that."

"Please stop. You are getting loud and people will hear you. You're making a scene. If Melissa —"

"If Melissa hears, she will leave you."

I couldn't believe she said that so fucking loud.

"You will meet me in the bathroom at one-thirty."

"Here… in your house? Are you serious? We have always been discrete."

"How about the bedroom? Maybe we can keep the door open a little and Melissa can watch. Maybe that vanilla wife of yours will get turned on and join in."

There had to be a dozen people around us in the kitchen that heard Jen say that. People were chatting but looking at us strangely; Melissa was in the other room. I don't think I have ever been more upset with Jen but didn't know what to say. I bit my tongue and stared at the clock. It was barely past one. I walked away from the kitchen looking for Melissa and saw her mingling.

"There you are, I was looking for you."

"I was chatting with Mark's sister Carolyn. Did you know Mark was a writer?"

"No, I did not." I was quite bewildered from the news. We had shared everything.

"Did you know he wrote poetry?"

"Melissa, I told you I didn't know he wrote. I wouldn't know what type of writing it was." I snapped at her. Melissa looked at me for a moment before she turned and walked away. I stood in a group of people and no one would look at me. I felt awkward and out of place.

I walked upstairs and could see Jen in tears. I could see her blonde hair up in a bun wearing that black dress, standing in front of the mirror. It looked like she had cried for weeks. I didn't know how we were going to have sex with her this way. I walked fully into the bedroom.

"Are you ready to fuck?" she slurred.

"Jen, we don't have to do this."

"You didn't have a problem taking advantage of me when I was in tears telling you he was diagnosed with cancer."

"Well, there was that one time before he was diagnosed, I drove you home after a wedding because you were drunk. Mark was out of town that week. It was you that took advantage of me. Don't make it sound like it was all me that pursued this."

"That's your argument? I was **drunk**. You could have stopped me. **You** were the one that wasn't drunk. Don't you ever wonder if that never happened, we wouldn't be where we are now? I often wonder if I had been loyal and faithful to him, maybe he wouldn't have had gotten cancer. I feel like God is punishing me."

"Then why are we up here?"

"This is what you want, isn't it? Don't you want to bend me over, pull this dress up and take you what want?"

"No. I don't."

"Jason, you are an asshole! You never once have had the courage to stand up to me. I have owned you in this relationship. It was always me that called the shots. It was always me making the arrangements and you listening like a little boy. You have never once wanted to stop this at all. You don't love Melissa. You don't give a shit about her at all."

"Jen, that's not true."

"Okay, then kiss me and let's continue this crazy fucked-up affair."

"Just stop. We can't do this here. I have an important question to ask you. Did you know that Mark was a writer? He never once told me that."

"Yes, I knew that. I honestly never read of any of his stuff, but I have always supported him."

"Jen, he never once told me that and I'm kind of bothered by it. In all of the years that I have known him, he never acted like it was important to him. I thought we were close and shared everything."

"Well, I can't speak for him. I can't explain that."

"Did he ever publish anything?"

"Yes, he told me he published a few books. Some of his friends really loved his poetry."

"I wonder why he never told me."

"We should go back downstairs now."

"Jason, look at me. What are you thinking about? Do you still want to leave me over a fucking sandwich?"

I finished the beer and glanced at her.

"I don't know anymore. Our marriage is such a mess. You won't go to counseling. You say you love me but your actions don't say that."

"Jason, just because I'm not a porn star in bed and not all over you all the time doesn't mean I don't love you. We have our differences at times, but I don't think it's worth throwing our entire marriage away. There are other reasons to end a marriage."

"Perhaps."

"Look at me; you view sex like a movie. I need an emotional connection and a certain kind of intimacy to be in the mood to even want sex. Only once in a while am I willing to be the woman you want in bed. But you want that all the time."

"Perhaps."

"Do you remember what happened the next weekend?"

All I could do was stare out the window.

"Jason, do you want another beer?"

It infuriated me that Mark never shared with me that he was a writer. We had been friends for over twenty years. Never once did he even express that and I just don't understand why he couldn't express that.

"Jason, are you going to ignore me?"

"I'm not ignoring you, I was just thinking about Mark. I guess it bothers me he never shared with me he was a writer after all the years of our friendship."

"Are you sure he never once told you?"

MELISSA

It's always about you. It's always about what I don't do and you making a damn list of it. I am the dumb ass who sticks around. I keep believing that you will change and love me for me. You must think I'm a dumb bitch and not see that you're fucking around with your best friend's wife.

"Actually, he did tell you, you don't listen."

"I listened to him."

"Jason, do you remember what happened the next weekend?"

Jason simply ignored me, like typical.

The week was normal. Every Tuesday and Thursday he would say he was working late. Maybe he was but, in my heart,, he was fucking Jen. I never did care for her. I could tolerate her. I just saw her as a pretentious up-tight money-hungry slut. The weekend after the funeral, Jason and I offered to help Jen with whatever she needed. Of course, she didn't want my help but wanted his help to move stuff from the house. Their house was always immaculate and organized so I don't know why she really needed help. I do remember I tried to make that Friday night special. I texted him around lunch time.

Jason, when you come home from work, come to the bedroom.

Hours went by and I never got a response. I called his work around three o'clock and they said he had used vacation time and hadn't been there. I was pretty fucking irritated.

I heard the door open and of course I could hear him go into the kitchen.

"Jason, did you get my text?" I hollered from the other room.

"No, I didn't. I didn't get a chance to look at my phone all day. It was such a hectic day."

"Well, I made plans for us. I made reservations at a restaurant downtown at seven. So drink that beer and hop in the shower."

If he had actually worked and responded to me, I would have attacked him in the bedroom just like he always wants but since he lied: fuck that!

He took off his clothes like normal and threw them in the corner. I could hear him as I was getting ready.

"Why are these books on the bed? Who in the hell is Chase Burrows?"

"I told you yesterday, don't you remember?"

Of course, he didn't answer me because I knew he hadn't been listening, once again. "Why are we going downtown? That's going to be expensive."

"I'll tell you at dinner."

— — —

"Look around at this place. You didn't tell me to wear a tie. Everyone is completely dressed up."

We finally sat down, and he seemed preoccupied.

"So, what's the occasion?"

"Well, remember that job I always wanted? Wednesday morning my boss told me organizational changes are being made and today he made it official. He gave me a huge raise, 10k. I now make the final call on whether a book should be published or not."

"That's awesome, dear! I am so proud of you!"

"Thanks, Jason. That means a lot. So are you helping Jen tomorrow?"

"Yeah, I told you I was. It's only for a few hours. I'll be home around noon and we can do whatever you want. Any thoughts on what you want to do?"

"Well, since I got a raise, and I know you've been wanting a new TV, I thought we could do that."

"You get a raise and you want to buy me a new TV? Aren't I just a lucky bastard?"

I watch him happily cut into his steak and just smiled on the inside.

"I can drop you off at Jen's in the morning. I have to work for a few hours anyway. Does that sound good?"

"Yes, that sounds good."

We went home that night and Jason glanced at those books again on the bed. I had never seen him read a single page of a book. Ever. Strangely enough, though, he actually picked one up and read something from it. I can even remember the poem he flipped to out of the book – "September Cries."

September Cries

She loved the morning
But she didn't love me
She slept with the dark
As she cursed at my name
Infidelity and lust entwine
Leaving my heart into dust
A month of sorrow
Discovering new shadows
Infliction and confliction bends
Torn in the veins
She loved the plastic
Shiny objects of nothing
Working for things
Greed sitting on her tongue

Swallowing emptiness
A lifetime of dreams
Turning into callous nightmares
Autumn leaves turn crisp
Cold as her icy skin
Betrayal broke me
September bellows
Fragments and pieces
Shake the trees inside
Love left me a long time ago

I remember Jason reading that poem and commenting on it.

"This is really good. It speaks to me."

"What is the author trying to say?"

"It sounds like love left him in the month of September. Like someone cheated on him."

"Would you read more of him?"

"Probably not."

I remember picking him up the next day at Jen's. She ignored me as usual but was giving fake pleasantries. I remember distinctly asking some questions.

"So, what did you help Jen do today?"

I asked this in front of them both.

"He helped me move some heavy boxes to the car. I went through some of Mark's things that I just couldn't look at anymore."

I am sure they made some time to have some kind of sex. I was eying them up and down. I was looking for "sex hair" and for any piece of clothing to be out of place. I didn't see anything. When we left, I asked him to drive.

"So how are you feeling – I mean, you have not said much about Mark's passing. I have not even seen you cry. He was your best friend."

He paused for a minute before answering. "Well it just sucks. Of course I miss him."

"How can you not cry then?"

"Not everyone needs to cry, you know. People handle emotions differently."

All I could do is think that he was handling it by continuing to fuck his best friend's widowed wife, even after he's gone.

I leaned over as he was driving and placed my hand on his thigh, I slipped my hand up his shorts and began to massage his limp cock.

"Melissa, what are you doing?"

"I am doing what you always want me to do – taking initiative. Do you want me to stop?"

He was completely hard when I asked this; I slowly stroked him.

"Melissa. It's during the day, someone is going to see you."

"Do you want me to suck your cock or not?"

"That's up to you."

I removed my hand and was so fucking irritated with him.

"Are you serious? Did it ever occur to you that I want you to say that you want it? Once in a blue moon, I want to be your slut… just not all the time."

That moment just showed me he would rather have Jen than me. I can't do anything to show that I do love him and want him.

"Melissa. I wouldn't have stopped you."

"WHY COULDN'T YOU JUST SAY, 'SUCK MY COCK'?"

All that ran through my mind was that Jen had already sucked it. He didn't see what he was really doing to us. We were no longer in sync emotionally, physically or sexually. The complaint was always as I heard it: 'you don't make an effort in our relationship'.

"So let's go back to the original comment you made, do you want our marriage to end? Do you still want to go to your brother's house?"

"I don't know anymore," he whispered.

I stared at him for a moment and I unleashed a deadly smirk.

"Listen here motherfucker, you are the most oblivious self-centered Sam-Adams-drinking piece-of-shit on the planet."

He startled, interrupted from his own thoughts. "What did you just say?"

"You heard me. Today is the day your glass world is about to shatter. I know you have been fucking Jen. I'm a smart fucking woman. On top of that all this time you claimed to have been close to and best friends with Mark. But you only know what you *want* to know. You never paid attention to Mark, not really. He was a soulful man. I have read all of his books."

"Why didn't you say that you read them?"

"You were too into yourself and fucking his wife."

Jason's face went completely white at that moment.

"It never occurred to you to connect any dots? I am the Chief Editor for a publishing company and have been publishing his books all this time. The one thing you actually read of his you liked; does the name 'Chase Burrows' ring a bell?"

He reflected a moment before recognition crossed his features. His face went whiter.

"It gets better Jason. He *knew* that Jen was fucking you. His relationship with Jen was no better. See, he loved his wife, he saw issues in their marriage, but he never made her feel like she wasn't enough. All *she* cared about was the lifestyle and money. And when he was diagnosed with cancer, she spent even more. Somehow he managed to keep writing and sending me the manuscripts."

Jason looked up at me in awe.

"So, are you going to leave me?"

"That's an excellent question. Actually, I am *not* going to leave you. Mark and I had an arrangement. Leaving you is too easy. You'll need another beer for this… You might even turn into an alcoholic and I don't really give a shit."

"Just tell me Melissa."

"There were so many times I tried to initiate sex with you but again you just didn't notice. So, to start off, I'm going to call a friend of mine that's been hitting on me. He is going to come over and he's going to fuck me with you watching. All those nights you claimed to have been working late it ate at me that you were having sex with Jen. You are going to be on the other end and see what it feels like."

His jaw dropped before he threatened: "I can leave you."

"You *could* leave me, but I will *bury* you. I will take you for every penny. All your friends and everyone you know will learn that you cheated with your best friend's wife while he was *fighting cancer.* I mean, how fucked up is that?"

I went and got his beer for him.

"So, I'll be a slut for someone else wishing you were him."

I went to the closet and pulled down a book that I had hidden.

"Mark wanted you to read this. Don't you love the title? *'The Cancerous Affair.'* You can find out what killed Mark, the affair... or cancer. Have this read by the end of the month. We can discuss it then." I leaned in close, our faces inches apart. "You are *my* bitch now."

GÖTTERDÄMMERUNG

by M. Ennenbach

One by one, the lights in the gray house across the street turn off until the entire house is nestled in darkness. A quick glance around the neighborhood shows similar results, as if as the midnight hour tolls from the church in the heart of town, everyone has the same ideas of sleep. There are no cars driving up and down the quiet street, no sounds emanate from the sleepy houses that line Superior Street. The entire area seems like it was snatched from the Fifties, white picket fences surround each home with small flower gardens and even the occasional tire swing drifts lazily from a gnarled branch of an old oak tree.

Not a single thing seems out of place in this picturesque scene of suburbia to the casual glance. But if you were to strain your eyes against the semi-cloud-covered moonlight, you might detect what appears to be a solitary form huddled in the bushes outside of the little gray house with the number hanging above the door. If you continued to stare at the silhouette in the bushes for a moment longer, you would notice it stand upright and stretch muscles that have cramped from an hour of motionless wait. And if you watched for a moment longer still, you would see the shadow quietly open the front door of 1312 Superior Street and shut the door just as quietly behind it.

The inside of the house is much the same as the outside: inside the foyer lies the living room with a nice, if not worn, couch that has a hand-knit quilt hanging over its back. An old rocking chair sits openly, as if inviting someone to come sit and rock away the stress of another day. Pictures line the walls around the fireplace with warm smiling faces looking down at the stranger who recently let himself in. The mantel of the fireplace showcases a large photograph of a couple happily sharing their first kiss of wedded bliss and is surrounded by photos of groomsmen and bridesmaids all sharing the couple's happiness. Another group of pictures shows the same two lovers on white beaches playfully frolicking in the rolling ocean surf.

The shadow steps up to each photo and stares intently at them, soaking in each detail before moving on to the next. For a moment the cloud cover breaks and pure moonlight bathes the room and the shadow reveals itself to be a man dressed in all black. He walks around the room with confidence as if this isn't his first time inside. The way he looks at the people that smile at him, it seems he is a friend or possibly family member just glad to be home. But he is neither friend nor family, for all of the names that he has been given there have not been many men like him at all.

After absorbing the entire room, he continues his scenic tour into the kitchen. Ceramic hens and roosters decorate the small comforting kitchen. The smell of dinner still lingers in the air, though no sign of it appears anywhere. The countertops and sinks are clean, and all the dishes have been put away. Even the dishtowel that hangs from the handle of the oven door is fresh and dry. He walks around the room deliberately until he reaches a set of drawers next to the double stainless-steel sink. Without hesitation he opens the third drawer from the bottom allowing the light to play across the blades of a full set of Ginsu knives.

He was there the day she bought them. Standing silently at the mall as she listened to the sales pitch. It excited him to approach her. The scent of her perfume filling his nostrils as the hunger raged in his head. He appreciated the heady irony of stepping up to her and pushing her towards the purchase with a smile and a tale of cooking for his family. She swallowed it too, hook line and proverbial sinker. He wonders if she felt electricity as she first unboxed them. If she knew what the blades would be used for one day. He smiles, imagining she did even though he knows it is impossible. *Or was it? Was anything truly impossible anymore?*

He stares at them for a moment, with that grin of memory, and silently pockets the long serrated bread knife then pushes the drawer closed. Opening the refrigerator door shows the remains of the night's feast safely locked away in a Tupperware bowl, a half-used gallon of milk that hangs precariously close to expiration and a carton of Winston Light 100's. The light from the refrigerator reveals the extent of the faux-country feel of the room; the hens and roosters stand by old fashioned metal milk cans and washboards. A small sign above the sink says, 'God Bless this Mess' and might have drawn a chuckle from anyone else. A large cowbell hangs on the wall next to the stove and attracts his attention with a small sigh of satisfaction. Using deft fingers, he quickly removes the clapper from the bell and gingerly takes it down from the nail on which it hangs and weighs it in his hand the same way a merchant might weigh a bag of gold during a business transaction.

Done in the kitchen, he makes his way to the stairs that lead up to the second floor of the house. The pictures that line the stairway don't quite have the joyfulness of the ones on the mantel; in fact, they almost glare at him with stark disapproval at his very presence. With the grace of a cat, he slinks noiselessly up the steps and down the hallway before stopping in front of a half-opened doorway. He breathes deeply as if catching the scent of the woman he knows will be lying asleep inside this room.

He stays still remembering coming into this house before; sitting on the couch downstairs and watching the television, grabbing a small snack from the fridge, and then coming upstairs to take a quick nap and absorb her scent. He knows the woman sleeping in this very room is alone, in fact has been for the eight months since her husband passed away from an allergic reaction to an immunization shot he got on a trip with their parish to Thailand.

He knows she fell apart and removed all the crucifixes and religious items from the house in her moment of crisis. She was the angel in her husband's congregation, the one pure being in a room full of sin. When the word of her husband's death reached her lovely ears, she was no longer an angel; she was instead a mere shell. And he watched her the entire time as she picked the pieces of her life back up and finally regained the will to go on. He saw her return to the church her late husband had given sermons in every Wednesday and Sunday and watched as she ran out of its doors with tears streaming down her face and cursing God for taking her husband away from her.

He followed her to the grocery store and restaurants, and even made conversation with her at the laundromat. He closes his eyes and remembers the force of his erection pushing against his khaki pants as she opened up to him and softly began to weep on his shoulder as she told the story of her dead husband. How could she have known he had been at the funeral as she threw herself onto the coffin as it was lowered into the ground? That he sat masturbating in his car as her black dress pressed tightly against her body while she pounded on the lid and begged him to come out of the box and home with her. Just remembering these events makes his heart pound and breath quicken, so he takes a few calming breathes as he prepares to open the door the rest of the way and see her sleeping face.

He knows he is unremarkable. Forgettable. Has been his entire life. The thrill of contact is heady like the sweetest bouquet of a fine red wine breathing on the counter. How many times had he started himself to approach her? The stories in his mind to explain another chance encounter at the ready but never needed. She would look at him blankly, no hint of recognition on her face. He sometimes wanted her to recall him. A flush of embarrassment at this stranger she had opened up to finding her again. That feeling of fate in every random meeting. But there was nothing, her eyes had long gone flat and dead. But he knows he can rattle the light to shine for the briefest of moments. It is his duty. His own personal mission. One he has trained for so long to fulfill.

The door squeaks as he pushes it open the rest of the way, but he knows this was coming and so is prepared for it. With a fierce stride, he makes it to the edge of the bed just as her eyes flicker open, curiosity at the noise winning out over sleep. Shock enters her gaze as he kneels quickly on both sides of her, causing the covers to act as a truss in which to keep her down.

"Hello again, Iris. Remember me?" he asks as a grin spreads across his face, and his hand covers her mouth, muffling the scream that was building inside of her. "It has been a while hasn't it? A shame we don't have the time to reminisce isn't it?" he says as he brings the cowbell down against the side of her head with an awful thud. Like a cobra, he strikes her again and again until he is sure she is quite unconscious. The cowbell in his hand begins to dent and a small amount of foam bubbles up from her lovely lips which tells him it is enough, and he sets the bell down on the nightstand next to her glasses.

He stares at her, watching the way her body convulses slightly and rubs the ever-growing bulge in his pants. She is even more gorgeous now than he remembered, and he hurriedly pulls down the covers to fully gaze at his catch. Her long blonde hair framing her plump face and spilling down onto her flannel pajamas, a slight trickle of crimson makes its way down from her right temple, drips onto her pale white throat before disappearing into the nether regions of her flannel top. He leans down and opens her eyes so he can gaze into the beautiful blue orbs which had called to him on their chance encounter at the beach. He remembered being lost in thought and accidentally tripping over her as she watched her husband swim in the ocean. Her eyes bathed him in the warm currents and he could feel himself drowning in them as he muttered a hasty apology and continued down the beach.

"You do remember me, don't you Iris?...You don't have to answer me, just lie back and relax. I knew you were the one for me that day on the beach, Iris. And then when we talked in the laundromat... I couldn't get you off of my mind. I wonder, did you think about me again after that day?" he speaks in a loving way, and a gurgle rises from somewhere deep inside of her and he smiles as if that is the answer he expected. "Now I am not going to lie to you, my love; this is probably going to hurt quite badly."

With this, he pulls the bread knife out of his pocket and methodically cuts her flannel pajamas, bra and panties off of her prone form. With supreme will he doesn't massage her supple breasts or even trail his fingers through her neatly trimmed pubic hairs. He feels the warmth of an orgasm course through him and he closes his eyes and goes with it. Whatever bit of life and will to survive she has reserved in her comes to force at that exact moment and her eyes fly open as her arms flail. With little effort he pins her down and stares into her eyes which now emanate hate and fear. He sees the silent questions of why and smiles at her as her expression takes on one of pleading. He feels her attempt to bite through the gloved hand over her mouth and he feels relief that he has waited so long to claim this prize. She truly has regained the will to live. Kneeling across her shoulders and with one hand across her mouth, he gropes down and finds the cut remains of her pajamas and tugs them out from under her. He ties her struggling hands together through the wooden bars of the headboard and slips a makeshift gag over her mouth. She bucks and fights and lets out shrill muffled screams as he ties each of her legs to a bed post. Deliberately he sits down next to her and stares deeply into her eyes and tries to give what would have been a calming smile under any other circumstances but comes off as almost feral under these.

"Iris, please relax and listen to me, this is all for your own good. Soon you will be heralded in Valhalla as a perfect Nordic Queen and the valkyries will cry for you as they enter battle. Just know that all of this was done for you, to help cleanse you of the sins of your heathen husband, Thomas," he says and watches her eyes widen and her struggles begin anew with determined strength. "You didn't know I knew your husband, did you? That I saw him force you to kneel at that heathen altar and pray to his god. I watched him try to turn you into one of the unclean masses and I knew he had to be stopped. I knew him better than even you, my love. I knew about his little trip to Thailand, I even knew how he lied to you and said it was "for the parish". But it wasn't for his false parish or his false idol; it was so he could have sex with little boys. Don't shake your head 'no' at me, I did it for you. He was a child molester and preached the foul gospel of lies to the masses and I did what was right for you and everyone else.

"It is quite surprising what you can get away with if you have the proper amount of money in Thailand," he ruminates. "You can get away with murder, if you play your cards right, or you can convince the man in charge of immunizations to inject a special cocktail and forge the death certificate to read 'allergic reaction'. And for you, my love, I would do it all again. I love you like your husband never did, like no one ever could. I love you enough to save you from this world and all of its lies."

Tears stream down her face and her muffled protests become sobs. He sits coldly, watching her cry while the love and longing erodes away and is replaced by rage and fury. *This is how she repays his love and kindness? He saves her from an eternity in Hell and opens her eyes to the foul lies her husband had preached...* He lifts the cow bell and brings it crashing down onto her temple and he feels the side of her skull cave in. He brings it down again and again until she begins to convulse and blood flows from her slack-jawed mouth. With one hand, he pulls open her left eyelid and stares into the blank orb, then with his other hand he reaches down and palms the bread knife again, places the tip against the center of her cornea. With just the slightest bit of pressure, the eye pops and a clear fluid bubbles up from the entry point.

He stares at it as it rolls down her cheek like a tear and across her full pouty lips. He feels anger again, but this time it is pointed inward at himself for losing control and ending the game before it could play out in full. He was enjoying playing with her; watching her face light up with pain and sorrow. Now he must be content with the knowledge that right before he crushed her skull, he has infused her with the thought that her dearly departed had been a child molester. That before he crushed her skull, he crushed her soul, sending her spirit spiraling ever downward into a dark abyss that light never shined upon. It was in his moment of great victory that his impetuous nature got the best of him and he hates it. But as he stares at the body on the bed before him, he knows that all isn't a complete waste.

With deliberate care he brings the knife lower and gently caresses the serrated edge against her nipples and then further downward to the tuft of blond hair that crowns her pelvis. He gazes longingly on that lone patch of hair for a moment and with a quick and savage move, digs the knife into her stomach just above it and swiftly rips the blade upwards to her sternum. It is such a quick slash that for a moment her body lays perfectly still, and the wound isn't even apparent, until suddenly the bright crimson erupts up and her chest opens like a rose in bloom caught on film and played in fast forward.

With a careful hand he reaches in, pushes aside the organs which held little interest to him and extracts the liver and spleen like a butcher removing the choice cuts from a slaughtered pig carcass. With one last longing glance, he turns and walks down the stairs and back into the kitchen, carefully carrying his two possessions. Left alone in the bedroom, the husk that once housed Iris seems to deflate as all the precious blood seeps deep into the mattress of her bed. It is as if she has sprung a leak, slowly draining away until all that remains is useless and cooling.

In the kitchen, he gently sets the organs down on the countertop and returns to the drawer that houses the Ginsu knives, rooting around until he finds the large butcher knife at the very bottom. With deliberate care and a keen eye, he splits the spleen right down the center and quarters it and then cuts again, making eighths. Pushing those aside, he grabs the still-warm liver and carves small strips from it until he has a rather large pile of pinkish-purple meat piled in front of him. Opening the cupboard door beneath the sink, he discovers a large skillet and with a little more searching, he finds some olive oil in a nice metal decanter, of which he pours a healthy dollop into the pan.

With great care to prevent burning the oil, he slowly raises the flame until instincts tell him it is hot enough. Well, perhaps it was less instincts and more all the hours of late night cooking shows on cable he finds himself entirely engulfed in. Once the oil begins to thin and spread across the bottom of the skillet then bubble ever so slightly, he places the strips of liver into the pan and adds a clove of garlic he found while peering through the cabinets as the oil heated.

Soon a terrific smell begins to fill the kitchen and he hears his stomach mumble protests at it having been so long since the last meal. He gingerly turns the strips over and allows them to sear thoroughly before pulling them up from the heat. One last trip through the cupboards has him grabbing a nice, if a bit gaudy, piece of china and some very nice, slightly tarnished silverware, which he sets into place on the table in the dining room.

In his mind he replays the way her blood flowed up and out of the slices he cut into her. He sees the shudders of agony and final struggles of life course out of her over and over again. He will replay this in his mind in an infinite loop for the next couple of weeks until another takes its place. Slowly, and savoring every bite, he finishes the meal and takes the dishes into the kitchen, washes them and puts them away. Going through the cupboards a final time, he discovers a box of plastic baggies and places the slices of spleen into one of them, making sure to seal it so the yellow and blue make green. Checking that the room is just the way he had found it, minus the cowbell and bread knife, he makes one more trip up the stairs to the bedroom. Standing still and taking one final mental snapshot of Iris and her empty husk, he blows a kiss to her before exiting the house back out into the night.

The empty street lined with dark houses surrounds him, but he allows himself to blend into the night. Anyone walking down the street will not even notice he is there, and even if they did intuit something amiss, by the time they turned around to focus in on him, he will be gone. In a matter of moments there is no trace that he has ever been on this street before, the single thing which gives away that anything has even occurred are the bright flickering flames rising, engulfing 1312 West Superior, rapidly burning the place to the ground and reducing the corpse inside to charred bone and ash. The police and fire trucks will arrive twenty minutes after the blaze ignited but by the time they will make it up the stairs and down the hall to the master bedroom and discover the remains, there will be no sign of foul play. The official report will state that the fire began due to faulty wiring in the master bedroom and poor Iris suffocated in her sleep. No autopsy will be performed, so no one will ever notice the lack of any missing organs.

He reads it all in the paper and smiles. The simple fire is something he prepared the first time he entered the home. It is amazing how easy it is to trigger an electrical fire in older homes, and he knows every way that is even possible. It simply requires an arc of electricity and the properly flammable objects nearby to catch the spark. With a few simple modifications in her bedroom, he has set up the Viking Funeral his beloved Iris deserves.

He smiles again as he carefully clips the article from the newspaper and places it into his scrapbook for safe keeping. His book is filled nearly cover to cover with clippings he has added over the years, each one remembrances of a soul he has sent to Valhalla himself. He lets his fingers trace along the print of the yellowing strips. A rush of smells flare to life in his head as the memories race through him. Jeanette, the buxom redhead with the long legs that seemed to stretch on and on. Meghan, the editor with the short hair and cats. Tara, all by her lonesome in Alaska with no one around for miles. So many happy moments frozen in time on every page. And this is volume three nearing completion. He wonders if their souls find one another as they sup in the Great Hall. Do they remember him as their savior? He closes the scrapbook and nods to himself. Of course they will.

Soon the Elysian Fields will call out his name and the Valkyries themselves will fly in to take his soul, but until then he has much work to do. And if there is any one thing he excels in, it is getting a job done right. The grin is still lighting his face as he sets the red bound scrapbook on the floor next to his bed. Unconsciously his fingers trace over the embossed letters which spell out the name he gave himself days past when he discovered his true calling: The Viking.

CHARITY

by Mark Ryan

TEA

The bell always irritated Mable. Tinkling half-heartedly whenever the door was opened. It, like the contents of the small shop, had seen better days. Its dull tin-thunking was only a sad echo of the once shiny and tinnitus greeting; placed there to alert the shopkeeper that someone had stumbled upon their small part of the town.

She sat at the counter of the small charity shop, her hands hugging a warm cup of tea. A huge cardigan was pulled tightly around her, the heating had been off again, and she dare not move for fear of the chill going through her. *'Such a draughty shop,'* she thought *'and that damn bell...there it is again!'*

"Morning Mable, how's it going dear?" A plump lady sang out, stepping inside.

There were just the two of them now; the last customer having left shortly before her arrival; empty-handed. *A time waster* Mable called them, those in to see if they can find something they can resell at a marked-up price. Discover some long-lost Turner masterpiece they can parade on television, reciting how they just stumbled upon it at the local charity shop.

Not likely. It was all crap in here. Huge bin-bags full of life's rubbish would be dumped at the front doors in the morning, people throwing out their old clothes that they hadn't bothered to wash. Used tissues and bits of food in the pockets, stains all over. She hated going through those bags.

"Oh Ruth, you know. Same shit, different day." Mable replied, sipping her tea as her explanation point.

"You've been at this too long you know; I don't know why you volunteer." Ruth said, coming across to the desk and popping her handbag on the counter.

"M'hearts too big I suppose," she replied. A cold pause landed and they both laughed aloud.

Both of the women volunteered their time at the MOCAP charity shop, a store outlet for a mental health charity which sold items donated by the public to help raise funds for disability centers. MORECRAP the ladies had humorlessly begun to call the place, not long after they both started there. This was an offshoot of the work they did for the Women's Institute in their small town of Gwendon, just north of Leeds. They had both lived there all their lives, putting in a good fifty years at the local biscuit factory before it shut its doors for good. Both now a bitter result of the years wasted making sweet treats.

For nothing but curiosity, Ruth was the older of the two, grown indifferent yet prepossessing as she hurtled into her eighties. Mable on the other hand was like a well-worn shoe, falling apart at the seams and eager to tell you that it hurts.

"Did you see what Doris put up there the other day?" Mable said, nodding her head towards the notice board over by the main door. Ruth turned to look across the shop, the layout of which was a cluttered bric-a-brac nightmare of junk with no defined sections. Clothes racks were rammed into corners; an old pushchair greeted you as you entered. Books and old copies of exercise videos were stacked precariously up the far wall giving Gwendon their own leaning tower. On the notice board, which was partially blocked by a wall of old jigsaw puzzles, many of which Mable had deliberately taken out pieces, Ruth could see a horribly florescent poster.

"What's this all about then?" Ruth said, waddling over to read it.

"Oh, wait and see." Mable replied, hunkering down and waiting for the reaction.

WI FESTIVE FAIR AND SNOW SHOW

DECEMBER 7th - 10:00am – 16:00pm

**Come along for Christmas cheer, festive cakes,
seasonal food stalls, activities for kids, face paint
and a snow display.**

**Talks and interactive sessions from MOCAP team members will give
you a greater sense of what we do at MOCAP and how we help those
with disabilities.**

Keep an eye out for one or two elves that might be about, sprinkling seasonal merriment and mischief.

Ruth turned back to the desk.

"You've got to be fucking kidding me," she replied.

"Nope, it's there as plain as day. And you know what, they want us all to be there to help out. They're getting some of the spastics in too, show off the courses or whatever it is they do. Snow show, if you please. I don't mind running this shop and baking a cake here or there. But I'm not babysitting and pulling tricks like I'm at the circus. It's a disaster waiting to happen." Another slurp of her tea.

"Well, I'm not doing anything if that Doris is running the show. She couldn't organize a piss up at a brewery. Why was this not sorted through the usual meetings? There's the luncheon the day before too, isn't there?" Ruth asked. She waddled back to the desk now, her face a display of disgust and annoyance.

"You know, I heard that...."

THUNKTHUNK

They both turned to see a small elderly gentlemen step into the shop.

"Good day ladies." He heaved, his old lungs struggling in the cold. A few flecks of snow followed him inside as he shut the front door.

Mable pulled her cardigan across tighter. It was Mr. Simmons again. He came in every Monday to see what new items had come in over the weekend. He would spend his time thumbing the books, reading aloud certain passages that took his fancy. He mostly bought clothes though, and Ruth recognized all the things he was wearing now had been purchased at the shop.

"Morning.' The ladies both replied, neither of them catching his eye which roamed quickly across the displays by the counter, engulfing the two old ladies and then on to the racks of men's clothing to the side.

"Any new stuff in my size?" he asked, making his way across to the rack.

"Gonna put on a brew Ma'bs, you want a fresh one?" Ruth said, ignoring the old man and heading off into the back of the shop.

"Nah, I'm fine with this still, ta." She replied. "Mr. Simmons, I've told you before I don't know your size, but there were some smaller items towards the back that might be suiting," she said, and flicked her hand at him, shooing him away. She slid off the stool she was on, feeling that chill that slipped in through the cracks near the door, and made her way around to a small display cabinet near the front window. She wanted to look busy, to avoid any conversation with Mr. Simmons while Ruth was out of the room. She could hear her now, the kettle chugging to life. They had a little kitchen just next to the small dressing room at the rear of the shop.

She absently picked up items in the display, chipped duck figurines and flower printed thimbles. Moving them from one side to the next while one eye darted to the clothes racks, hearing the snuffling of the old man like a hamster in a huge ball of hay.

"Mind if I try these on?" she heard from him after a few minutes. Turning she saw he was weighed down with numerous items, half of which she knew wouldn't fit.

"You know where to go," she replied, turning back to the little china figures.

Mr. Simmons made his way to the back of the shop, pulling across the pathetic little curtain that constituted a door to the dressing room. He saw the shadowy silhouette of Ruth on the walls of the little kitchen, the darkened weather outside forced all the headache-bright lights on in the little shop, many of the little corners in the old building throwing shadows that danced over the once treasured items.

He heard the kettle tick its completion and Ruth humming inside the kitchen area.

He pulled the curtain back. It was a small space, but he had ample room. His height had diminished greatly in his receding years, barely over five feet at his prime, the winter days of his life had him pushed smaller and smaller, adding a stoop now so as to move about like a small vole. He began to get undressed, making sure the curtain was tightly pulled up. One unfortunate occasion in a department store had led to accusations and contemptuous looks which had made him wary. He placed his shirt on the metal hook and unzipped his trousers. Pulling them over his shoes, which he'd left on.

A flash of white, and jets of liquid were funneling from some new source all over him. He didn't feel the pain straight away, caught by surprise by the figure of Ruth bearing down on him. She poured the hot water from the kettle all over his body, turning the greying skin to a brilliant red that hissed and fizzed. His heart paused, jumped to one final crescendo and collapsed much like his little body did, crumpled on the floor of the dressing room.

"Ruthie! Mind you don't get it on the carpet." Mable called, going over to the front door and turning the sign attached to 'closed'.

SCISSORS

The snow had begun to drift and pile outside the small shop, sneaking up to the storefront windows. The cold had ravaged the town for weeks now and showed no signs of relenting, covering everything in a festively white blanket.

Mable took her time walking up the high street to the shop that morning. Mindful to find the safer patches on the pavement where the grit laid down had clumped and offered more solid treading. Others rushed by her, in a shopping haste and of youthful disregard to the potential slippery path.

For a small town, Gwendon always seemed to be busy. The local market brought in people from miles around, and the shops never had an issue in custom. Their little charity shop was just off the main market square, its charitable statues providing cheap rates for a prime location. And surprisingly, was the only one in town. Mable knew of a place three towns over where they were blighted by nothing but charity shops and cafes.

She crossed the road gingerly and trotted the rest of the way before stopping for a moment outside the shop. She saw the Christmas decorations had been put up since she was in last. No doubt Grace had been busying herself with that. She loved that sort of thing. She liked all the holidays and the color, she was one of those people who were perpetually in a good mood. Mable suspected that when she was alone she would weep hysterically at it all, or at least be thoroughly miserable by herself. But no, she had surprised the woman a couple of times, finding that silly smile plastered across her face like it had been drawn on by a clown.

They volunteered in shifts; which was always a bone of contention for some of the ladies. Nine of them in total, with Patrick from head office who would come down once in a while and throw his weight around. *Patrick, the little prick.* Not older than twenty-five, he would come into the shop and linger unnecessarily all day. Blathering on about health and safety, asset management and the like. He was a bore and a prat, and Mable had little time for him. She didn't mind the rotating pattern of the shifts herself, it gave her a mask of flexibility in an otherwise dull routine.

The Christmas lights blinked in and out on the tree in the window. Crappy toys and stuffed animals littered the base, a makeshift tree with the unwanted gifts of yesterday. A wreath on the door welcomed her, and she noticed some mistletoe of the plastic kind had been hung up just inside as she pushed into the shop. *'That stupid cow.'* Mable thought.

Normally the shop was quiet save for the customers, but today some music was playing. An old cd player had been brought to life and was rolling out the non-offensive sounds of easy listening from a decade ago. She could still smell the new carpet, and she wiped her feet on the mat by the door so as to not damage the grand new flooring.

"Mable, thank goodness you are here. It's been madness this morning," came a voice and then a shockingly made-up woman in front of her.

"Daniella, you always think it's a crisis when you're on your own," Mable replied, stepping up the little steps and removing her jacket. She could see there were a few customers in. A few women gaggled by the clothes and a few more over by the toys with the kids picking things up and throwing around the toy animals.

"Oh, to tell ya'. First Mrs. Brady came in to pick up that jacket she had put by, and lord knows, I couldn't find it. Of course, that led to us to calling Dolly, she switched days with me if you remember this week, who had no idea what I was talking about. So, half an hour later....." Daniella began. She was a kind but frantic woman, dolled up to the nines with nowhere to be. She liked the drama and chaos that she could create, stopping only to fix her hair and recount the pressures of being her.

"Did you find it?" Mable said, knowing you had to cut in to stop her going on.

"Oh yes, we did. It was right in front of me all along." Daniella said, giggling. "You know me."

"Mmmhhmm." Mable replied. Hanging her jacket up by the counter. "I see the heating is fixed now."

"Oh yes, had to be. Had to be. Couldn't have us working here in the freezing cold. Mrs. Jenkins said she wouldn't come in no more if the heating wasn't fixed!" she replied, bobbing along behind her. "Wasn't that terrible about poor Mr. Simmons?"

"It was a shock, but accidents do happen." Mable said, opening the till to see how much money had been taken that day. A small portable heater blared next to her behind the counter, its hot air felt like a panting dog's breath on her legs.

"Yes, yes they do. There's been so many passings this year though. Only the other week Mrs. Russel was talking about..." but she was interrupted by a lady wanting to try on some clothes. Daniella smiled, and led the woman away, showing her where the dressing room was, her chatter now finding a new audience.

£48.36p

Not much taken that morning. *'Busy my ass,'* Mable thought. She watched as the kids were getting more boisterous over by the toys. One of them, a little girl, pushed over a board game box which landed on the boy's head.

Mable smiled.

The little bell chimed, and the sounds of the street followed by a lady with a pram, within which the child was doing all it could to cause a storm, screaming its little lungs out. Everyone in the store turned to look as they entered, the mellow sounds of the CD player almost extinguished by the cries.

"Come on, grab those things you want and let's get going." She heard the mum say to the kids who had been fighting.

"Ohhhhh Tracey, so good to see you, and little Mickey what a darling." Daniella sang as she made her way back towards where the woman with the pram was. The woman smiled, pushing the pram further into the center of the shop, blocking the way out.

The kids threw some items onto the counter in front of Mable. A puzzle game and a toy robot. The mum sighed, giving a half-hearted smile whilst digging into her handbag for her purse. Mable rang them up, placing the toys into a cheap market bag. The boy snatched it out of her hands suddenly. She scowled at him. The noise from the baby was getting worse, the cries reaching higher. Daniella's insistence on picking him up clearly had set him into another wave of screaming which shot through everyone.

"Here you are!" the woman buying the toys said to Mable, offering her the five-pound note. She shook it a little as she would a treat to a small animal. Mable took the money and gave her the change, watching as they quickly swept out of the shop and back out into the cold.

"Oh Mable, isn't he adorable?!" cooed Daniella, rocking the baby and looking over to the counter. She was oblivious to the fact that everything she was doing seemed to be agitating the child further. 'What a moron,' Mable thought, nodding over to her and Tracey; the woman who had a tired expression and vacant eyes.

"Precious." She finally offered. Opening one of the drawers to the counter, she reached inside. Her hands found the stickers quickly, and she took these and the pair of scissors out and began to make her way around towards the rear of the shop. She pulled out some of the boxes they had stacked up, and randomly started to fish out items that needed to go on the shop floor. The screaming got worse; Daniella had resorted to wafting a stuffed bunny in the child's face to calm him down. Mable could hear the woman in the dressing room sighing, equally annoyed by the incessant sound.

More people entered the shop. The baby continued to cry.

She grabbed some of the DVDs she had slapped a sticker on and took them over to where they needed to go. There were too many there already, but she was just going through the motions.

Tracey had begun to look at the costume jewelry they had in a small glass case near the counter. Patrick had been insistent on keeping the valuable items nearest to the counter. A dull light had been put inside the case in the hopes to illuminate the rhinestones. Instead it gave them a dulled look, like the eyes of dead animals that had been stuffed with sawdust. Daniella, giving up with the effort to entertain the baby through puppetry had now lifted him up again and was flying around like some spectral idiot.

Mable quickly plonked the DVDs on the shelf and walked over to where Tracey was, brushing closely past the pram which was stuck like a sore thumb in the center of the shop.

"See anything you like?" she asked the young lady not much out of her teenage years.

"Nah, not really. Don't know what I really want, to be honest." Tracey replied, pushing the strands of hair out of her eyes that had fallen down whilst looking into the cabinet.

"There are a couple of some nice pieces but come back in a few weeks if nothing grabs your eye. We always get the better stuff after Christmas." Mable said, smiling. Tracey half smiled in acknowledgement and the apathy of youth.

"Uh oh! I think someone has gotten too excited." They heard Daniella say behind them. Turning, they both saw her theatrically screwing her nose up and wafting her hand over the bum.

"For god's sake, I just changed him," Tracey said, going over and taking the child.

"You can change him here if you like, out the back." Daniella offered, her smile never wavering.

"Nah, it's fine. Best to get home and do it there. He'll just have to wait. Won't you, you noisy sod!" And she pulled the pram around and began to leave.

"See ya then," she said, making her way over to the door and out into the street.

The bell signaling her off.

"Yeah, you take care, dear. And you too, little man," Daniella said, standing in the middle of the room, clutching her chest as if bidding farewell to her own child.

"Isn't he a darling?" She said once she was gone.

"A complete terror." Mable snorted, sitting down again at the counter.

"Well, yes he was a bit out of sorts, but oh that little face," she added.

"I would be screaming too if that were my mother. Barely out of school herself, that one. What does she know about having a baby?"

"Well, she perhaps has made some questionable choices, but no one is perfect. And he is quite a darling," Daniella said.

One of the women who had been trying things on had sensed it was now safe to emerge and came to the counter with a bundle of clothes she now wished to buy. She didn't look poor, Mable thought, more like the type who liked vintage clothing but didn't want to pay the silly city prices for trends.

"How did you get on dear, everything fit okay?" Daniella asked the lady, who was still tucking her shirt into her jeans.

"Yes, I'll take these please. And this hat." She said, passing over a bobble hat with a severely oversized bobble on it. "But can you cut off the bobble, I think I'd prefer it without and I'll wear it now," she said.

"Of course, dear. Mable, pass me those scissors from the drawer please." Daniella said, holding out her hand expectantly.

Mable absently glanced into the drawer and then replied.

"They don't seem to be there anymore; they must have gone walkies."

CAKE

The Women's Institute, or WI as the renegades termed it, is a community-based organization for women established in the 19th century. Their reach is far and the objectives clear; campaigning for issues for women whilst fundraising and helping charities. Today, and in the little area of Gwendon, they specialize in cake sales and produce markets, raising funds and doing good in the community. Not solely restricted, but usually known for its gathering of older ladies; helping them help and also feel active; veiling a need for socializing.

With any society there is a hierarchy, and the WI of Gwendon was no different. As a group, they were an individual entity from the Woman's Institute as a whole, each person a committee member for the branch. But at the top was the chairperson, who in this case was a Mrs. Jackie Rutherford.

They were all a genuine bunch, kindly and helpful; the idyllic notion of growing old. Mrs. Rutherford was voted chairperson for the group consecutively year after year. She was a doer, and the ladies looked to her to lead the charge in their small society. Secretly she loved the little bit of power she had, and though the group was democratic, there was a foreboding sense that it would not do to change the top.

Ruth had once thrown her own hat into the ring for chairperson. She thought it might be fun and a change of pace. She had been unsuccessful, naturally, and didn't bother again. Instead, she and Jackie became very good friends over the years, Ruth becoming more of 'second in command', which suited her fine. With her time at the charity shop, she was glad to have some balance to her volunteering. MOCAP was heavily linked to the WI and they mutually benefited each other.

It was Thursday and grey outside. The snow had stopped but a silent storm now hung over the town. Inside the charity shop, the heating blared. Ruth had cranked it up fully and set up little portable heaters, causing a wall of heat to greet you as you entered. She hated the cold. She was placing things into the window display, adding to the festive charm, when the phone rang. She quickly went across to it on the desk.

"MOCAP charity shop," she answered. "Jackie, good to hear from you... What's that dear?... oh yes I'm here for the next hour or so... Okay, see you shortly," she said, hanging up the receiver. The phone often rung, mostly wrong numbers as they shared a similar one to the local leisure center. Mable was known to give wrong times and dates for swim and yoga classes.

The shop was empty at the moment and she went into the back to use the toilet quickly. It was small and grim, a pea green paint had unfortunately been chosen to adorn the walls, which boxed you in like a coffin. The back area of the shop was actually quite roomy compared to most. Patrick had been insistent on disabled access and fire routes and the like. Ruth hadn't minded all that nonsense as it gave them a nice little kitchen and room to move around. Aside from the toilet, of course. One of the problems, though, was the back alley, as that did tend to attract the rats, being so close to the river. The bins in the yard were a perfect dining experience for the water-roaming furry friends.

She finished up and returned to the front of the shop, going back to her window display.

It was about half an hour later that Jackie arrived, coming in the back of the shop. Ruth heard the car and the heavy fire door slam. Jackie liked to mutter to herself and Ruth could hear her now in the back struggling with something. She went to see what was going on.

"What's all this?" Ruth asked, noticing the boxes on the counter.

"Cake, like I don't see enough of them." Jackie puffed, slightly out of breath. She wasn't as plump as Ruth had become in her twilight days, but she smoked like a chimney and the years of lungs swimming in tar had caught up on her. She heaved another box onto the counter then stood back, rummaging in her handbag for her cigarettes.

"Cake and sandwiches. We've got that lot coming up from Manchester this afternoon." She said, now looking for her lighter.

"Is that today, I thought they were coming next month now?" Ruth asked, surprised. She lifted the lid of the bigger box, peering in to see the cake inside.

"They want to go through the Christmas charity expenses before the end of the year, so they've decided to come up today. All last minute of course. That twat Nancy Sanjdon called me yesterday to ask if we can arrange it for them. But get this..." she paused and lit the cigarette.

"Jacks, crack the door so it don't set the smoke alarms off." Ruth said, nodding to the back door.

"Oh yeah, sorry." Jackie said, going to the door and pushing it open. The cold December air rushed in and blew the smoke up towards the ceiling.

"They're going ahead with democratic suspension of voting in the new year now." She dragged on the cigarette.

"What! Really?!" Ruth replied.

"Yep, but we don't get to choose one of our own at all. No, no. They've got some bitch from York moving down to take over." Jackie was angry, Ruth could tell. And who wouldn't be. The WI here had always been self-sufficient, taking the commands from the wider body only when they had to. Jackie probably took these things as a personal attack on her way of running things.

"They're going over the coming changes this afternoon too." She breathed heavily out along with her smoke.

"That's awful! Who is it, do you know?" Ruth asked, a pattern of concern taking shape in her mind.

"Remember Katie Rivers from the general assembly last year?" Jackie said, a knowing grimace in her eye.

"No!"

"Uh-huh. Miss Brown-Noser herself. She'll be there too. Come to lord it over, I imagine." Jackie spat, the flavors of disgust in her mouth.

"Well, we'll have to speak up and formally complain. They can't just come along and…"

"The thing is, they can, and they will." Jackie puffed on her cigarette earnestly, sucking out the goodness like marrow from a bone. She flicked the ash out in the direction of the open door, most of it landing on the floor inside.

"Listen, I gotta do some errands before taking this lot up to the hall later. If you're free, do you mind giving me a hand?" she asked, glancing at the boxes of food. "Need to set up the tables and chairs, too."

Ruth looked at the boxes, then towards Jackie. She was weighing up the information and trying to judge how much the crest had fallen within her. The old ladies of the group weren't ones for change, though Ruth didn't usually mind. As long as the change came from their own hands.

"Sure Jacks, I'll be done here in an hour when Janet comes in," she finally replied, her mind now turning.

"Great, thank you! I'll see you then." And she flicked her cigarette out of the door; it sailed off into the wind and the great white unknown. She turned and followed her cigarette out, letting the heavy door slam behind her. Ruth stood for a moment in the kitchen area. She hadn't cared for Katie at all, and the thought of having to do as she said suddenly flared a rooted anger within her, setting free the hounds that usually took over when she let things slip inside. Jackie was a leader, one who got things done. She liked how she managed the ladies and she thought this was a bad rub on her, without any consultation.

So, she was quick and precise.

She kicked open the rat trap they had by the back door. The long plastic tube contained a little bit of poison that the rats would snuffle out, digest and go elsewhere to die. Ruth thought this poetically ironic as she broke off the sticker holder and emptied the poison into a cup on the side. The little blue and green pellets looked like colorful sugar puffs, and she made quick work of grinding them down with the back of the tea spoon that she had used earlier.

The cake was a modest affair, a freshly baked Victoria sponge with fresh cream filling instead of the usual buttercream. The strawberries on top seemed out of place in the wintery season, it conjured images of summer fetes and lazy days by the river; odd in December somehow. The cream and vanilla sponge looked awful light in texture compared to the ground poison pellets. *'Annoying'*, she thought. *'A chocolate one would be easier to hide it in.'*

But needs must, and she lifted the top layer clean off, sprinkling the fine powder all over the cream; her little dustings of death.

Taking the spoon she used previously, she whipped the cream around a little more to conceal the powder, dropping the top layer back onto the cake to conceal her crime. She knew Jackie would not eat it, she was allergic to strawberries, and wasn't the biggest cake eater anyway, if truth be known. She hated all the cake sales and judging festivals, spitting out many mouthfuls over the years in the WI that she remembered. No, she would be safe, but the others were in for a surprise.

The time came later when Janet arrived to take over at the shop. The customers that day had been drab yet frequent, the till was bursting, and Janet noted that it had been quite a week already at the shop. *Christmas,* reminded Ruth; *some people can't afford brand new presents.* Jackie returned not too long after, and they both made their way to the hall to arrange things for the coming meeting. Ruth was finally done around two-thirty, stopping in at the Co-op to pick up a few groceries on her way home. She treated herself to a cake for when she got in. A nice chocolate one, her favorite.

— — —

The hall was cold and many of them shivered for the first half of the meeting. The large room took ages to heat, though the heating had been on for nearly an hour beforehand. They always had meetings in here; the old guildhall of the parish was ideal for council sittings and formal meetings such as these.

They took a break midway through. Jackie calling for thirty minutes after the accounts and charity expenses had all been resolved. A change in the plans meant there was an obvious absence in the room, one Jackie had noticed right away. It seemed alterations had already descended on the plans for Katie Rivers to relocate and take over the chairpersons' role. In an ongoing re-assessment of WI structure, things would remain the same now while a new strategy was devised. Jackie prided herself for being able to cut through bullshit, and she was able to wrangle the truth out of one of the other members of the committee. Too many people had complained about the proposed changes across the regions it seemed; there had been an uproar. For now, the shakeup plan was dead in the water, and Jackie was free to continue where she was; swimming in her own contentedness.

They finished the teas and the sandwiches, many of the salmon ones were left and pushed to the side. With the change in agenda, the meeting would now be finishing a lot earlier than planned which Jackie was very pleased about. The afternoon session would take the form of general catch-ups and Christmas planning.

"The cake looks lovely, Jackie. You not having any?" Cathy Rhimes asked, slicing off a huge chunk for herself.

Jackie, fresh with her good news and lighter afternoon, felt happier and relaxed.

"Oh, go on then, I'll pick around the strawberries. Maybe just a small bit with lots of cream," she said, licking her lips.

FIRE

Patrick loved what he did. He felt like he was making a real difference in the world. He fully believed in MOCAP and what they did for disabilities and helping the less fortunate. He had sought out a charitable body soon after he'd finished his degree, eager to get moving in his career and help where he could. He knew the work they did actually made a difference to people's lives. Patrick's road was paved with good intentions, good ideas and some might say, idealisms. If criticisms were to be thrown at him, the biggest one would be that Patrick was a bit of a know-it-all. Second to that would be his unfortunate inflated sense of importance.

Patrick's job within the organization was to site manage all the charitable outlets for MOCAP for his region. This meant he was responsible for all the charity shops they operated, all event spaces they hired, and all facilities used; they needed to be safe and up to standard. Not his standards, mind; he'd come to learn quickly that his bar was a lot higher than those set out in legislation. He was there to enforce all of this and keep everyone safe and working.

One of his favorite parts to his job was onsite inspections, though he liked to call them 'drop ins'. He would usually try to arrange these every other month with all the sites, which was ambitious to the wide ranging scale of his region. Not only did he get to catch up with those who volunteered at the shops and address any problems face to face, but he secretly liked how he was treated when he got there. Most of the shops were run by aging older women, and Patrick had one of those boyish faces which made the old dears fuss and croon over him. He could hold their attentions and they would fly about when he would suggest something, so desperate for his approval and trying to please him. He loved the adoration, and thus, loved his site visits.

All except Gwendon.

That wasn't to say he hated going there, he still got to go dispense his extensive wisdom, but there was just something off with the branch. Some of the women would not swoon or welcome him or his advice. Indeed, some seemed positively resentful for his being there at all. Mable made him feel like he was something she'd stepped in on her way to the store. So quick to wipe him off with disgust.

He never knew why. He would always be jolly, smiling at them when he came in. He'd learnt all the tricks to manage people and how not to be patronizing; to be genial and engaging. He knew their names and addressed them respectfully. But for some reason, a few of them just didn't want to get on board.

This again was how he found it, visiting the Gwendon branch a few weeks before Christmas. He'd parked in the alley behind the shop but came around to the front entrance. This was more polite and also gave him a chance to risk-assess the building from both sides.

The bell above his head tinkled as he stepped inside, a wall of heat hitting him as he entered.

"Good morning Doris, how are you m'lovely?" Patrick said, eager to take his jacket off due to the heat.

"Patrick, you're right on time. I always like a chap who is punctual." Doris said, pushing her huge glasses back up her nose. She was a tiny woman and she barely reached above the counter. She was so small, in fact, that once someone had mistaken her for a large doll in store. Doris was prone to zoning out and would stand motionless at times, staring into space.

"Always good to be on time. Just you today?" he asked, nodding across to a customer who had turned to see who had entered also. They quickly went back to browsing the racks of books, running their finger along the spines as they mouthed the titles.

"Oh, my no, Mable is in the back. She's just making some tea. Would you like something to drink?" Doris said, shuffling forward now to see him.

Patrick's smile wavered for a moment. He could hear the tink-tink of a spoon hitting a cup now from the kitchen area.

"No, I'm fine dear; had something on my way over," he replied.

"You didn't drink in the car, did you? You know you're not allowed to do that. They'll catch you and put points on your license if you're not careful." Doris said, concern across her face now.

"I was careful, don't worry," he said, taking off his jacket.

Mable appeared at the doorway then at the rear of the shop. A huge stuffed owl was propped on the shelf right by the door, its expression alive with fright. It and the huge spider plant on the other side framed her now as she paused in the doorway like some alternate Botticelli tableau.

They locked eyes for a moment, Patrick being the first to look away.

"Ah there she is, the savior of the refreshments. How are you Mable?"

"Fine, yourself?" she said coldly, popping the tea for herself and Doris on the counter, sploshing a little over the sides of the cups.

The bell tinkled again, and an old man entered the shop, nodding to the ladies before beginning to browse the items by the front window, making his way deeper in to the shop as he went.

"I'm fantastic thank you. You both looking forward to Christmas this year?" he asked them earnestly. He began to fumble in his bag, looking for his notepad, which he would be needing.

"Yes, I suppose so. Comes around so soon, and so regular." Doris said, somewhat absently. She was watching the old man who had come into the shop, tacking his movements as he went from one display to the next. She watched him like someone would watch a bag caught in the wind, mesmerized and apathetic at the same time.

"Course you'll be here for the Christmas fair, won't you Patrick?" Mable suddenly asked. Her eyes, much different from her colleagues, burned into him.

"Pardon me?" Patrick asked.

"You know, the Snow Show. The festive fair. My bet is, you'll be one of the little elves running around sprinkling us all with festive joy and sparkle." Mable said, drier than sandpaper. Doris's eyes widened.

"Oh yes, the show. That *will* be something. How many of the spastics will be coming, Patrick?" Doris asked.

"Now Doris, we don't like to use that word. They are just *handicapped*," he replied.

"Oh. Sorry then," she said, not really seeing the bother.

"And there will be quite a few people coming along. We've got a few buses organized to bring everyone down along with the team leaders and carers. And yes, I have been asked to dress up actually Mable, but I'm afraid I won't be able to, as I need to leave around lunch time." he said, somewhat defensively.

"That is a shame. But you'll be there though, won't you, keeping everything safe and structured?" she added, trying to tap at an unseen button.

"Yes, I certainly will be. Now, getting to what is safe and structured," he said, putting his bag down by the counter and flipping over his notepad. "I've come to check on a few things here, and update you on certain changes in legislation," he started.

Mable rolled her eyes and muttered under her breath, "For fuck's sake"; which Patrick didn't hear.

Another customer entered then, the spark of the cold air from outside rushed on through, and they turned to see the woman enter. Patrick nodded and greeted her, reminded by the wall of heat that had greeted him when he entered.

"Now, firstly. I know it's very cold outside, but it really is quite warm in here. We do have certain thermostat levels you should be using, and I notice there a lot of heaters dotted around the place. Have these been PAT tested?" he asked them, clicking the pen he'd also retrieved from his bag. He was getting very hot now, he could feel the sticky heat under his arms already.

"Ruth got those heaters, not Patricia." Doris offered, taking a sip of her tea for the first time.

Patrick sighed.

"No, not Pat, P-A-T. Portable Appliance Test. The electrical devices need to be tested before you can use them here. It's all standard operations. Remember the manual I gave you all at the beginning of the year, it's all in there," he said.

"That thing, don't even know where it is." Doris replied innocently. She had the nature of a lovable, but stupid, pet. His smile wavered. He noticed Mable just staring at him, like he was a strange creature to her. Some other thing that had come in and won't shoo away like the customers.

"Right. Best to start from the beginning then. I'll take a look around and spot check and we can then go through the procedures again. If you could look for the manual, I'll make a list of things you should check and do each day, try to make that easier for everyone," he said, loosening the top button to his shirt.

"If you like." Doris said and smiled over to the woman who had entered and was making her way across to the counter. "Those are lovely, dear," she said, reaching out to take the flowered Wellington boots from her.

The bell rung again and they turned to see Ruth enter the shop with two other older ladies. One of them was dressed in a large fur coat and sported a very small hat upon which sat a huge pink flower. She was small and very thin, the giant coat swimming around her. The other wore light rain gear, mismatched and with odd outdoor hiking clothes. She clutched a huge handbag, the type some people use for travel bags. She, like Ruth, was a little bit plump; they came, in single file, into the store whose space was getting filled up very quickly.

"Good day ladies." Patrick beamed, nudged accidentally in the back by the lady wishing to buy the Wellingtons.

"Hello young sir." The lady with the fur coat said, pulling up the collar slightly. The other one said hello also. Ruth moved a bit closer before saying anything.

"Patrick. So nice of you to drop by; it's been a while," she said, casting a glance around the shop. Then introducing the women, "This is Geraldine and May." She did not indicate which was which; like Mable, she kept her stare on Patrick and did not offer to suggest who was who.

"Didn't I see you once before at the harvest festival?" May asked. She was the fur coat wearer, and she took off her hat now, letting her greying hair fall down to her shoulders.

"Urm. I don't think so." He said, knowing he hadn't been that year.

"May. Patrick is a very busy man, he can't go to every event we do. No, I don't think he was here for the festival or maybe only there for some of it." Mable suggested, smiling slightly which seemed odd on her face.

"Aren't they lovely?" Geraldine said, noticing the Wellington boots that Doris was selling. The lady buying them smiled back at her. "I could do with a new pair myself you know. Reggie and I are looking after June's dog in a few weeks, and I don't like this weather. He's a runt of a pup, but June adores him. I'll need something better than these things to be out and about in," she said, kicking her foot forward showing off a well-worn pair of hiking books. The lace on one shoe was coming undone and part of it lay on the floor like a small snake.

"Well ladies, I will get out of your way. Things to do and all." Patrick said, jostled from behind again by the woman at the counter.

"Yes, dear. Don't let us stop you." Geraldine said.

"You been offered a drink Patrick?" Ruth asked him, noticing the cups on the counter.

"He didn't want one." Mable said, bluntly.

"Yes; no, it's fine. But thank you. I'll be in the back if you need me." Patrick said, and started to make his way further in, noticing how many of the little heaters were dotted about the place. They were old, and he could smell the burning metal as he passed one of them. He left the ladies at the front of the store, hearing them begin a flurry of talk and conversation. He caught the drifting chatter about food poisoning before moving back deeper into the store.

He noted on his pad the new carpet. It was a deep pile and was ill-suited for a commercial property. He noted the door to the kitchen area was propped open with an old metal Victorian iron. The route to the fire exit blocked by a stack of bags and boxes. The health and safety poster had random things stuck over it now, postcards and magazine cut outs, one a recipe for a spinach and potato quiche. His little notepad was filling up quickly as he made his way to the storage cupboard. This he knew would be shambles but to his surprise, it was neat and orderly. The little cupboard was an odd space. It was narrow and split purpose. To one side they stored their brooms and mops, the hoover was careful packed to the left of the shelves on which they kept cleaning materials. On the other a guarded small flight of steps led down to the old coal cellar from when the building used to be a miner's cottage. He was surprised the light was on down there and he ventured forth to inspect the lower level.

He went down the steps and could see the well-lit space below. Old MOCAP display boards were stacked to the sides, and a mannequin stood in the corner, one of its arms missing. Boxes of old stock and bits and pieces littered the floor but were stacked neatly. The general use for the space was for storage, but in the center of the room there was a table which had stacked upon it a number of portable heaters. Old ones and some new, some looked like old fire grates, others were like small lamppost lights that would glow orange like fiery braced teeth. Why there were so many here he didn't know, but he knew they weren't safe to use, none of them having been tested; just like the ones upstairs. Most of these, in his opinion, should be thrown away due to how old they were. He wagered they had used these in the time the heating was off, bringing in the ones they perhaps had at home to make do.

He switched off the light and made his way back up to the shop, the light thrown from the open door calling him upward.

Ruth and Geraldine were in the kitchen area, the kettle was boiling away merrily, and he could hear the shop was quite busy now with customers. *Midday rush most likely*, he thought.

"There he is, we thought we'd lost you." Geraldine said. She stood next to Ruth who was popping some loose-leaf tea into a huge ceramic teapot which sported a hunting scene; a little hare being tracked by hounds.

"Just in the cellar inspecting," he said, closing the door behind him.

"Why do you need to go down there? Surely, it's the shop that needs to be safe, not some dingy old coal cellar. Besides dear, it's mighty dirty and gloomy." Geraldine asked.

"He has to check everywhere; it is part of the job." Ruth said, going across to the small fridge to retrieve some milk.

"Exactly, and someone had actually left the light on down there, so it is a space that is in use. Can I ask why there are so many heaters on the table there?" Patrick asked.

"Be a dear and grab that biscuit tin out of the cupboard next you there Patrick." Ruth said, nodding towards the bank of cupboards above him and ignoring his question.

"We have to have the heaters in the store, the main heating hasn't been working properly. It's been frightful cold lately." Geraldine said, tipping the water now into the teapot. The steam and the smell of fresh tea lifted up, steaming up her large glasses that perched on her nose.

"Yes, but why are there so many downstairs? You don't use all of them, do you?" he asked.

"There aren't any down there. The ones we have are in use around the shop. Like Geraldine says, we needed them. It gets bloody freezing in this old building." Ruth said.

"There are dozens of old and new heaters on a table downstairs. You shouldn't need to use the heaters anyway as the main heating is working, I hear the pipes now creaking and churning away. And you shouldn't be using the heaters that haven't been tested. But the ones downstairs are so old they are a real fire risk if you use them." Patrick said, getting frustrated now.

"I don't know what he's talking about Ruth. Couple of heaters to keep the old dears warm. What's the problem?" Geraldine said, putting the lid on the tea pot.

Mable entered the kitchen now, bringing the empty cups from her and Doris.

"Right then, come with me and I'll show you the heaters downstairs."

"The heating controls aren't down there." Mable said, putting the dirty cups in the sink.

"Not the heating controls, the heaters, stored on the tables." Patrick replied.

"There aren't any down there." Mable said, cool and calm.

"For fu….Fine. Come with me and I'll show you," he said, opening the storage cupboard door and flicking the light on that was at the top of the small steps.

"I'm not going down there, not with my back." Mable said. "I'll take the tea, you two go," she said to Geraldine and Ruth.

And so they followed Patrick down the stairs into the old coal cellar.

— — —

The light above them begin to flicker as they eventually found themselves at the bottom of the small stairs. The old cellar was surprisingly warm; one of the heaters had been plugged in in the corner and had been coughing out its little heat. The old boiler was down here too, and Patrick had failed to see the source of the warmth previously.

Ruth and Geraldine followed close behind him, commenting on the light which was now buzzing intermittently above their heads.

"There, you see. Look at all those heaters." Patrick said, triumphantly.

"Oh, you meant these old things." Geraldine said, walking across to the table and seeing the old heaters. She diverted and went up to look at the mannequin in the corner of the room. "Ruth, remember this old thing? We got it from the old Price's department store years ago. Oh, they used to have some lovely dresses there. You can't get them like you used to now."

"Course she's seen better days, this one." Ruth said, going across to where she was and pulling the remaining arm up and down.

"Ladies, please. The heaters." Patrick said. The boiler in the corner seemed to flare, stoked by an increase in temperature request no doubt.

"Who's turned that thing up? They can't be bloody cold up there, it's already a million degrees!" he shouted, clearly frustrated.

"You young ones don't feel the cold like we do. It is snowing outside you know, Patrick." Geraldine said. She was digging around in a box next to the mannequin now, fishing out some odd bits of clothes that had been left there.

Ruth went across to the table where Patrick stood. She glanced at the heaters on the table and then said indifferently. "We like to keep warm Pat, is that a crime?" Her face was taut, but Patrick could read the smile beneath the façade.

It is sometimes the little things that set people over the edge, and there, within the smile that wasn't a smile, lay the final straw for him that day.

"That's it, I've had enough of this. You've all been lying about these fucking heaters, and here they are plain as day. You don't even need this many, it's a pokey little shop not Albert Hall. They are unsafe, and they are to be removed off-site this instant!"

"I don't care for all that 'fffy-fffy' Patrick," Geraldine said, shocked by his outburst. Ruth continued to watch him, to see what he would do next.

"They are safe anyway." Ruth said, seeing how far she could push him.

"Really? Well let's test that theory, shall we?" And with that, Patrick grabbed one of the oldest looking heaters and went across to the plug socket near the boiler. He wrestled with the cord which was fraying at the end, and with great resolve, plugged the heater in.

Geraldine came over to where Ruth was standing; she clutched some of the old clothes she had found in one of the boxes.

"Patrick, what is the issue here? Who cares if they work or not?" she implored, concerned by his change of manner.

"I CARE!" He yelled back at her. The heater had sprung to life, the old contraption groaning into a red hot little furnace.

"Those old ones always did ignite pretty fast." Ruth said as they stood watching the little glowing heater.

Tick tick tick.

It was the boiler stoking up further, the thermostat upstairs being pushed up a few more degrees.

"Are you kidding me!" Patrick yelled out, watching the little pilot light on the boiler flare into a blue supernova.

It happened suddenly then, a few sparks began to spit from the wall socket. The frayed plug wire began to sizzle as the firework rain tumbled down and began to ignite the cord. A few more of the sparks spat out and landed on some of the boxes nearby. Geraldine panicked in all the pyrotechnics suddenly going off around, she flailed her arms in the air, stumbled forward into Patrick, dropping the clothes she was holding onto of the little old heater.

They went up like a roman candle.

Flames spat out and began to dance all over the cellar. Geraldine rushed to the stairs while Ruth watched Patrick a little longer, urging him to do something; perhaps forcing him to weigh in on all his talk on health and safety over the years. A fire blanket and extinguisher were fixed to the wall on the other side, and he made a dart for them as Ruth made one for the stairs.

"Go, call the fire brigade and get everyone out of the building!" he yelled. Ruth was already halfway up the stairs and she flew up the rest with great speed, defying her plump stature. While battling the flames which were starting to engulf the boards and boxes, Patrick did not see the door being closed at the top, and above the roaring flames would never have heard the lock turning in the latch.

— — —

The shop burnt down of course, that is to say, a good part of it. Firemen sifted through old Dolly Parton vinyl records and charred tableware, books with their dust sleeves burnt away and a mountain of spoiled clothes. They found two people still alive however, both unconscious. They pulled Patrick out with serve burns to his right side, his right arm burnt to a degree that he nearly resembled the distressed one-armed mannequin before its untimely demise in the flames. He was taken to the local hospital, which was going through a renovation at the time. If conscious, he would have been very distressed at seeing all the health and safety oversights the building work was presenting.

Mable, they found unconscious in the kitchen area, near the cupboard door. She suffered severe smoke inhalation; her old lungs ravaged just a bit more after years of smoking two packs a day. She was hailed as a hero in the little circle of WI members, fighting against the odds to make it downstairs and help Patrick trapped in the old coal cellar as it filled with smoke and flames. Little details always get lost in tales of heroism. Truths sometimes get in the way. That she was found holding an industrial bottle of turpentine by the cupboard door muddies the water a little, so is usually omitted.

While the MOCAP shop is gutted and cleared, a makeshift charity sale is operating in the guildhall, where items can be bought for the charity and to raise funds for the rebuilding effort. Clothes and books are for sale, and you can also have some tea and cake there. Perhaps a nice bit of Victoria sponge, good in any season.

REVOLUTION

by tara caribou

Mark slowly came to awareness from a deep dream-filled sleep, stretching out his long limbs and scratching his side. He yawned in the dim red light of his bunk and flipped the thin wool blanket off his legs. Today was the beginning of the revolution. His revolution. He would start it or he would die trying. He couldn't find a reason to fully care either way.

He flipped the switch and the flickering yellow bulb overhead protested momentarily before giving in with a sigh. Shuffling to the washing alcove and standing at the sink in his tiny apartment, he felt the thrum of the generators through his feet. By now he was used to it, but something inside him told him it was wrong. It wasn't natural. They weren't meant to live this way. Pulling out his brush and crushed charcoal, he began brushing his teeth. The black flecks staining his lips and teeth the sickly grey had always fascinated him. He was both alive and dead, and the color reminded him of that.

As he went on with his daily routine, he remembered the day he found himself here. That morning, so many mornings ago, had started normal for a sunny summer day. He was nine or ten, he couldn't actually remember that part. Since school was out, he woke without an alarm and quietly pulled on a pair of moderately clean shorts and a rumpled t-shirt from his bedroom floor. He tiptoed past mom and dad's bedroom and made his way outside. There was a creek at the end of their street and he spent most of his waking hours there when he wasn't back home grabbing food or checking in with mom. Even now, he wished he could remember their names, his parents. But kids never cared much for things like that and here he was years later wishing he at least had that part of them to hold.

He recalled tossing sticks into the creek and trying to guess which would reach the little waterfall first. He recalled the sun warm on his back. He recalled the sky turning a bright crimson fading to purple and feeling overwhelmingly tired and a pressure behind his eyes. Falling to his knees and sleeping. He recalled waking up in an unfamiliar wood with a sky that was a little too lavender and a smell that smelled just a little off from what he had always known. *He now knew the smell came from the Worker Class and their strange unclean ways.* Back then, he just knew that he wasn't home anymore.

Mark spit out the grey mixture of saliva and cleaning charcoal then rinsed his mouth out with tepid water that always tasted old and musty. He knew it shouldn't taste that way, even if it was all he could remember the taste of at this point. He didn't exactly know how long he had been here or even how old he was. The people here didn't have "calendars" like his people did. They didn't have timepieces of any kind. They did things on the schedule of the Keepers. Everyone ate when told and worked when told. No one here had ever heard of a "birthday" or "Christmas" or "weekends." Morning was when your alarm chimed and night was when you slept. But words did little to connect with the actual flow of days as he remembered when he lived on his own world. No one left the building to watch the sunset or sunrise. No one watched the stars. They served no purpose, so why?

He didn't know how long he'd been here but he did know he was an adult now. He had patchy black whiskers growing on his chin and had for a long time. He knew adults had hair growing on their faces. Dad had a beard. It was always kept tidy and clean. And there were little patches of white and grey in it. He wished he could remember the color of his eyes though. It's strange what you remember and what you don't. He remembered dad smiled a lot when he looked at mom but rarely ever laughed. He was always dressed fancy when he left for work and he always came home at the exact same time every day. But he couldn't remember his dad's eyes or his name.

Splashing water on his face, he relived those first days in this new place. He had sat up in an alien forest. He appeared to be on a wide trail of sorts, thin vines and grass wrapped around his arms and legs loosely, like a soft cocoon. Soon he heard talking. Looking about he finally saw them round a bend. There were four of them. A large rabbit, probably two feet tall. A mouse nearly as big. Something that was like a dog, it took him a while to remember they were called bulldogs. And then a badger. He didn't know if it was big or little, it was about the same size as the others. It wasn't their size that was as remarkable as the fact they were talking and that he could understand them.

The four animals stopped when they noticed Mark sitting there, gently unwrapping the foliage from his limbs. They exchanged glances with one another. The mouse dropping its head and shaking it while muttering, "not another one". The rabbit hopped forward a couple hops closer and turned its head in a peculiar way, looking him over. With a single nod of its head, he stretched forth one paw and said in a kind voice. "Where are you from, friend?" "You.... you can talk?" had been Mark's reply. The rabbit glanced back at the others and then at him again. "We can talk. But it's not safe here. You shouldn't be here. You don't belong here..." The bulldog interrupted, "we need to leave. You know what happens next, if they find us." The others nodded in agreement.

"Wait!" Mark called, as the four turned to leave the way they came. "Where am I? Who are you?" The rabbit only shook its head sadly prophesying, "I'm so sorry you have come here. It shan't be easy for you now. No not at all." Then turning, the four made their way swiftly back down the trail. Whispering amongst themselves and clearly in a hurry to put distance between the boy and them. Mark pulled his knees to his chest and wrapping his arms about his legs, began to cry softly.

He had stuck around the general area all that day, exploring very little, hoping that the creatures would come back and explain things to him. As evening fell, he began to get a little scared. Not of the dark, but of the unknown. He missed mom. He was hungry. And he was alone. Sometimes he thought he could hear whispers at the edge of his hearing but when he called out, there came no reply. Then just as the first stars began to appear, he heard a "psst!" nearby. Looking about himself, he caught the white stripes of the badger. "Psst!" it growled again. Mark crawled over to it. "Follow me," the badger whispered. He did as he was told, moving quietly as he observed the badger doing the same. Shortly they came to a small rock wall and at the base a narrow entrance to a cave. It quickly grew dark as they navigated deeper into the cave but Mark had put his hand on the badger's back and trusted it enough to continue following it through the cave.

Minutes passed before they suddenly halted. There were the sounds of a key turning in a lock, followed by a dim light flooding the narrow passageway as the door was pushed open. They crossed the threshold and closed the door behind them. The badger sighed with audible relief. "I'm sorry for all the secrecy but these are dangerous times in our land and I am sorry that you have made your way here to witness it." It busied itself at the small fireplace, adding a few more logs and stoking the flames up a bit. Then it lit a few oil lamps and gestured for Mark to sit on the rug in front of the glowing fire. Reaching into a small box, the badger removed a sausage and a wheel of cheese. From an open cupboard, it pulled out a round loaf of bread and set all three things in front of him. Mark ate nearly all of it before his hunger was tamed. The badger handed him a small flask which it said was thulaberry wine. Mark didn't know what that was, but it tasted a little like grape juice soda only not as sweet.

The badger sat in a worn wooden rocking chair and lit a stone pipe, the white smoke curling as it rose to the ceiling, which Mark just now realized was dirt and he could see a few roots poking down into the chamber. He scooted a little closer to the fire. A few minutes passed before the badger spoke again. "I brought you here because I read in my leaves this afternoon that I was to bring you here and give you the Seeing Herb. This is all I know or can tell you. The herb will tell you the rest. I wish I could let you sleep first but I really don't know how much time I have." It motioned with a claw to a small shelf above the mantel. On it rested an ornate clay box. Mark pulled it down, briefly noticing the intricate green leaves and flowers inlaid within its surface, and handed it to the badger, who opened it and pinched a small grape-sized clump between its claws. "Chew on this, don't swallow. Chew until there's nothing left. Swallow the juices." Mark did as he was told, completely trusting the strange creature. The dried plant, which he noticed was a blueish green and appeared to have golden threads coming off it and covered in silver crystals, tasted like the forest and something more. An almost bitter flavor without being off-putting. He chewed and chewed, swallowing his spit when he needed to.

At first he had felt a pleasant peacefulness fall over him. This was followed by a clarity in his surroundings. He noticed the different colors of the dirt floor and ceiling, the flames of the hearth casting dancing shadows, the smell of the badger's pipe. Trinkets and bottles and dried flowers rested upon every available ledge. His gaze was drawn to the badger's whiskers as it puffed on its pipe, eyes closed, until looking up, where he watched the smoke gently curling above their heads. He lay back, arms crossed behind his neck, and watched entranced.

The smoke began to move in different ways and he found that he was seeing shapes which materialized into definite forms and then complete scenes. He watched as if a movie played before him unfolding. And he learned.

— — —

Mark startled from his reverie as a knock came at his apartment door. He spun the hatch wheel and tugged inward, the drawn-out groaning creak protesting its use. The door had always stuck just a little, giving away its ancient age. Once when he had still lived in his own world, dad had taken him on a tour of a coast guard cutter boat. At each separate section, you had to step through a special door that they called a hatch. He remembered the uniformed guard explaining that it was so they could perfectly seal off the areas, should an emergency come about. It was the same thing here. Hatches to protect. Or so they were told. It had always felt like it was hatches to control.

Outside his door stood Praefect Himmon, dressed in the tailored suit of his order. They were meant to appear as the "common man" yet failed to do so in that no one wore tailored clothing except the Keepers. Nor did anyone wear such soft clothing. Power indeed came with privilege. Mark performed the necessary hand sign acknowledging the praefect's office and authority and bowed slightly.

"Come." Praefect Himmon said, then turned and shuffled down the corridor, knowing Mark would follow. Mark pulled his hatch closed and followed, passing dozens of doors just like his on their way. At times they would cross or turn down an intersection and one could easily become lost in the monotony. It was dim within the metal-grated corridors with a small orange light pathetically glowing every five doors. Periodically a tiny map of the building would appear on the wall to guide any lost souls.

Within minutes the two men arrived at the lift which would carry them to whichever level the praefect decided he would work on for the day. Sometimes it might be the garden levels where the food was grown and from which fresh air was pumped to supplement the stale air of the lower levels. Sometimes it was helping in the large halls where the people ate in shifts. Sometimes it was cleaning or repairing in any one of the many many rooms of the building. The Keepers didn't seem to care if someone didn't like performing a certain task or if they were better or worse at it. Everyone rotated doing different jobs. It was the one small break in the tedium of it all. Once more, Mark was flooded with the thought that they weren't meant to live this way. And *this* was just a small part of why he must begin his revolution.

"Today, we need you topside," the praefect intoned. Mark turned toward the older man to acknowledge him. "The Piggurls are squealing again. They respond to you. Deal with it and clean up the mess." Himmon paused, scrutinizing the younger man for a moment before continuing. "You have always fit in well with us. We notice. You will be rewarded. I don't need to remind you do not believe the things they say. Piggurls have their place among the people, just as you do. We all have our parts to play." Mark noticed the look of righteousness in the praefect's eye as he spoke. *'He actually believes what he is saying,'* he thought. Outwardly, he nodded and then, "I understand, Praefect. I am for the people." Then bowing once more, he spun the door's hatch and stepped over the threshold and into the bright light.

— — —

The Keepers never came topside. It was too dangerous, they said. What if one of them fell off the edge? There were so few of them to keep the order of the people. No, they always sent others out.

After Mark left the badger's den that night long before, he slowly forgot all he had seen through the ingesting of the special herb. His young mind, in the following days and years had chalked the incidence as that of the imagination of a young boy. It wasn't until somewhat recently, a few hundred shifts ago perhaps, that everything had altered for him.

The change for Mark had started one shift when it was reported that somehow the Piggurls, the creatures who lived in the very bottom levels and who were the ones who kept the machines which powered the building running properly, had managed to climb up the many many levels up through the ventilation shafts all the way topside. It was a fight to contain them. The vile creatures squealing out that they weren't made to live like this, slaves in a hostile environment. Even as they were tossed over the edge of the building or skewered with the metal spears the Keepers had ordered the small numbers of people to defend the building with. Still they had squealed about the dangers below. The horrible ways they died every day. The disease. Mark had heard them even as he fought them. One had run up to him, eyes wild and covered in weeping blisters. He grabbed her, and her skin sloughed off in his hands as she slipped right out, bloody ruts where his fingers had dug in. "Save us!" she had squealed in terror just before one of his comrades rammed a spear through her open mouth out the back of her head. He had looked at his hands and saw her skin covering them. He had looked around him and saw what they had done. He looked and memories of scenes within moving smoke began to form.

Shortly after the uprising had been quelled, and grating welded to the top of the ventilation shafts in order to prevent another such event, Mark had been assigned for ten shifts in a row to work down on the only level moderately shared by the Piggurls, also called the Worker Class when the Keepers spoke their indoctrinations out, and the rest of the people. The Piggurls were not allowed to leave their work areas, and the thick doors had long ago been welded shut to keep them there. But there was an area where the new Piggurls were created in their incubators when more were needed. And more were always needed. A request had been sent to the Keeper's offices that the mechanism which moved the new babies into the Piggurl's level had jammed in some capacity and was not functioning properly.

Mark had entered the lab expecting at least one other person with him but found himself alone. He got to work on the ancient mechanism which had locked up. The work required help from the other side of the gate, and so it was that he met his first Piggurl. 'Met' wasn't quite the right term. They never saw each other face to face, but instead spoke through the video intercom. The creature was disgusting in appearance. She stood just over a meter tall, with squat bloated features. Her eyes were too close together and shaped more round than a person's eyes. Her nose was flat and looked more like a snout than a nose. Her head was too round and a little too big sitting on an almost imperceptible short, thick neck. Her skin was rough and covered sparsely in long bristly hairs. She suffered from the disease of her people, which caused their skin to nearly melt from their flesh.

But she was methodical and intelligent in her work and within a few hours began to speak freely to Mark. He offered little by way of return conversation, as he cared very little for such things or even for the creatures themselves, responding with one-word grunts, if anything at all. Occasionally interrupting her constant talking with instructions relating to their job at hand. He tried not to look around the lab where the little babies lay in various stages of growth. They didn't look human. They looked like animals. It made him somewhat uncomfortable, so to ease his mind, he found himself really listening to the pitiful thing on the other side of the wall.

She told him why they had climbed the shafts. She described their terrible disease, one which shortened their lifespan to far less than they knew it should be. Because of this, they had a rich oral history maintained as they had told themselves they would not forget their origins. She was part of a small group of her people who decided they would not live this way anymore. They wanted freedom. They wanted to live outside of the building. They knew through tradition that at one time their world wasn't just a building on the water. That people walked the land a long time ago. Mark stopped her: "Buildings on water?" "Yes indeed," she snorted. "Didn't you know? Long ago your people lived on the land and made food grow in the soil. But somewhere along the way, they came up with a power source which killed off the growing land. The other creatures of the world who had once been your allies rose up and great battles broke out and your people were almost exterminated when the planet itself seemed to fight against you. A short truce was made giving your people time to make buildings that could be on the open water to which they were banned. The problem is, you didn't keep your word. You kept the fuel source to power your buildings and at some point the Keepers realized that it was killing you. They created a disposable creature to maintain the engines. They mixed humans and wild pigs together and here I am, working for you. I didn't ask to be created, but I want freedom for my people. I want to be able to cure our disease."

Mark realized his hands had stopped their task and he picked a tool back up. A memory had formed in his mind of a badger in a den and shapes in smoke. Could it be? Was it real after all? At that very moment the horn sounded which signaled that his work quota was done for the day and he was to make his way to a food hall. He switched off the video-cam and climbed into the lift. To say he was troubled barely described it. He felt a righteous light flare in the back corner of his mind; justice must come for the planet and broken promises.

The next eight shifts he heard so much more. He didn't want to believe what she said but he felt the truth of it all. The third shift, she told him she had something for him. Sending a small box which fit in the palm of his hand back through the conveyer hatch, he opened it to find it full of a dried flower or herb. The smell of it brought memory immediately rushing back into his mind, as it was the same flower he had chewed in the badger's den long before. It was in that moment he realized for certain it hadn't been a dream. He looked at the video-cam, "why?" "Chew a little when you're in a safe place, maybe before you go to your sleep shift." "I don't understand." "You will."

As he lay in his bunk that night, Mark pulled out a flower and pinched off a little, remembering what the badger had told him and began to chew it carefully and swallow the juices only. He felt weightless. He closed his eyes. He dreamt he stood in a circle of trees. Within that circle was a circle of bushes. Within that a circle of grasses. Within that a circle of flowers. And within that a circle of mosses and him in the very middle, his bare feet in rich dark earth. "Help me understand." He heard whispers. 'We have brought you here from your world to save us. You must stop the people from killing our world. We are dying.' "Why me? How? I don't understand!" 'Listen and learn.'

And so it was each shift he listened. And each sleep shift he chewed the flower and slept with visions. Somehow, the very plants themselves were able to communicate with him. He saw the history of the world unfold as they saw it. He saw a time of peace between the planet and the many peoples, including the rabbits and badgers and dogs and pigs and mice and so many others. Some he didn't recognize but many that resembled those of his home world. He saw the people who began to rape and pillage the land. Not being the good stewards they were meant to be. Instead selfish and reckless. The people took advantage of the animal-people, forcing them into slavery. They poisoned the land and the water. Then there were wars. So many battles. The land itself began to fight against them. Opening up and swallowing whole armies. Flooding their villages and food sources. Then as they were pushed to smaller and smaller areas, they began to hold flags and cloth as a sign retreat, begging for mercy, a treaty was made. The planet allowed the people a set time to build great ships to house the remaining people and they were to discontinue all use of their poisons and live wholly on the ships. There were originally twelve ships. Two had not survived and had sunk out of sight. The other ten remained.

The people did not hold to the treaty. They continued to poison and weaken the land. In its distress, it brought others from his world here in an effort to stop the evil from within. Mark had been only one of many. The planet was becoming weaker. The men from the ships were leaving and landing on the nearby shores, stealing and pillaging. The animal-peoples were becoming more scared. Becoming wild. Putting less faith in the land. But the plants, the flora themselves, were dedicated to ending this. Mark was one of the last chances they had. Mark felt Destiny in his heart. He cared not for the people. Nor the hybrid pig-humans. Nor the animals. He did care for the planet and the plants which had reached out to him and pulled him here, placing Faith in him. It was for them he would rise up.

Then it was on the tenth shift that he was greeted by a different Piggurl. When he asked what happened to the one he'd been working with, she responded with a dead-eyed snort, "The disease took her." And though he felt nothing for the perished Piggurl, for she had served her own purpose, still Mark finished his task fixing the mechanism with only one thought on his mind: he would end this or it would end him. On the intercom, he reported to the praefect on duty that his task was complete. "Were the Workers compliant?" "Always." "Excellent. You may return to quarters until it is your meal." The screen went blank. Mark did as he was instructed, and a plan began to form.

— — —

And so it was today that everything had aligned and brought him here, topside, his revolution itching just beneath his skin. The bright light of the little-too-red sun made him shield his eyes for a moment before they adjusted. He heard the snorts and squeals of the Worker class beneath the grating of the ventilation shafts. He strode purposefully over to the nearest vent. Looking in, he saw the ugly faces of three of the creatures. "Are you ready?" he asked. There was no hesitation, "we are." "Where did you hide my weapon?" "Vent 4A." Mark glanced over his shoulder to the named vent and nodded once. "Human." He turned back to see the dirty fingers of one of the Piggurls latched around the grating. "Many of us will perish, but we are all perishing," she whispered. "Thank you. You aren't one of us and yet you were brought here to listen and save both our peoples from destruction. Before you go into battle, take this." In her other hand she held three small leaves pinched between two of her thick, hoof-like fingers. She poked them out between two of the bars. "It is the power of the land. It will fight with you." Without a word he took the leaves and again nodded. He knew they were already aware of their own part in the uprising.

Standing up, Mark walked to the edge of the building. A moment of clarity, a memory of his past life perhaps, dropped into his mind and he remembered it was called a ship, on his world. He peered over the edge and looked down, far down, past levels and levels of living quarters, past the growing level on down to the bottom two stories that housed the generators which poisoned the world while powering the ship, tended to by the engineered Piggurl people, not quite human and not quite beast. A disposable product for a species that cared nothing of the world around them and the affect it had. Lifting his eyes, he looked out on the dirty water that they had long ago been condemned to, spying maybe eight or nine ships like this one. All releasing the toxic waste to the water below. All of them killing the world they used. All of them needing to be taken down. He could hear the squeals of the creatures which he knew filled the ventilation shafts. The anticipation was thick and palpable.

The first thing Mark did was pop the grating off of the vent that held his weapon. It was a key fob of some sort. He didn't question how the Piggurls came to obtain it, only that they had. It was engraved with the mark of a high-ranking praefect. Perfect. Next, Mark pulled out a small welding torch from his pocket and got to work cutting the welds off the nearest shaft. Once done, four Piggurls pulled themselves out and taking the torch for themselves, went to work on the next shaft, quickly releasing their people to fight a battle they knew they would perish in.

Striding over to a storage box near a door, Mark opened it to find a long coil of rope, musty with age and lack of use. He reached down and checked to make sure the long knife he had stolen from the food preparation area shifts ago was secure in his boot. Finding it to his satisfaction, he made his way to the edge of the ship and walked along its edge for quite some distance away from where he had entered, moving nearly three quarters of the way to the front of building. Or what felt like the front. Upon reflection, he mused momentarily, it could be the back. But somehow he felt the Keepers would be in the best parts of the building. Peering over the edge, he could see where there were open bays a few levels down. According to the Piggurl, the

Keepers were the only ones that had large flats which also had open-air balconies. Mark had never seen or heard of one, but he felt it to be true and here was the evidence. He looked about the deck and found the only suitable stationary object to tie off to was a door's hatch handle. Perhaps that would work to his advantage, in case anyone from within tried to come out this door, it would at least slow them down.

He sat near the edge and waited, giving the Piggurls time to do what they also needed to do. Pulling the three pale yellow leaves the Piggurl had just given him from his pocket, he looked at them momentarily before placing them in his mouth without hesitation. They seemed to stick to his tongue, almost like they grew little spikes. It didn't hurt so much as startle him, though it was uncomfortable. He realized he couldn't move the leaves from his tongue to chew or swallow them. They had a mild almost sweet peppery flavor. Not overbearing, but present. And then it happened. He felt a life-force, a power not his own flood his body. His mind seemed untouched. Or was it? As he looked around himself, it was as if he could see in new colors. He could see where life grew and what was inanimate. Small bits of lichen or mold almost glowed. He realized he could *feel* the life. He felt life stirring in the decks below him. He could feel the Piggurls further down the deck. Their anticipation. Their righteous yet stupid anger. He felt other Piggurls much further away who felt almost nothing. Dead-minded. When he concentrated on a ship on the horizon, he realized he could feel life there too, though fainter. He smiled.

Some short time later, he knew the Piggurls waited. They were ready. So was he. He put his hand down to push himself up and moss grew instantly there. His eyes widened in surprise. He wondered what else the planet would help him with. Grabbing the rope, he wrapped it carefully about his legs and waist then slowly rappelled, walking his way backwards over the edge (no hesitation) and down the wall. Two levels down he came to an open balcony. It appeared unused, as the furniture was all turned upside down and was a bit dirty. Perfect.

The window of the apartment it was attached to let him know it was dark inside. Trying the handle, it opened freely. Inside he found the apartment was indeed empty. Against the wall he saw a screen and he walked over to it. Touched it. Immediately it lit up and a list displayed. Most of it made no sense to him because his room didn't have the same type of computer. His had two channels. One showed vids of various speeches Keepers had given in the past or public service announcements. It showed times when the Keepers may make appearances, gracing the children's area or in the eating halls. Shaking hands. Smiling. Waving. Blessing. The other channel had entertainment on it. There were interactive card games or fix-it games or how to cook games. Either was just as bad as the other, in his opinion. But this screen wasn't the same. It had a place to sign-in assumedly for a personalized experience and then there was a schedule of events and a map and....he selected the map. He needed a praefect's office. Navigating the screen wasn't too difficult and he quickly found the nearest mid-ranking praefect. It was surprisingly close. He looked at his feet and noticed grass growing there.

Opening the door, he carefully poked his head out. Didn't see anyone or hear anyone. He paused. He needed to be prepared. He reached inside his boot and pulled out the kitchen knife. Felt its weight in his hand. Then slipped out the door and headed for the room he needed. He passed a couple doors where he could slightly hear noise from the other side of the room. It sounded like parties, with laughter and screeches and other wild sounds. He kept moving. They would get their time. Upon reaching his destination, Mark silently checked the door handle, only just now noticing that they were not hatches, but actual handles like from his home world. The door opened. He stepped in and heard a man speaking quietly in the next room. He readied his knife, walked in without preamble. "What the--?!" the man exclaimed, clearly startled as he attempted to stand but Mark stretched out his arm and vines shot from his fingertips, covering the man's mouth and wrapping instantly around his face. The corpulent older man's eyes grew wide just before Mark unceremoniously slit his throat.

He walked back to the front door and locked it, then went to the praefect's vid screen and got to work. He used the fob to gain access to more programs on the computer. Moving quickly, he found where the parts that controlled the air shafts and locked doors was, opened them. All of them everywhere. In the distance, he heard klaxons. And now the Piggurls would begin their part.

— — —

Mark wasted no time. He would take down the Keepers. As he made his way out of the praefect's room, he noticed an ornate ceremonial-looking knife. He paused before the case. Intuited that it was in fact from his own home world. He wasn't sure how he knew, he simply did. It was beautifully carved and when he broke the glass and pulled it out, knew the weight and balance was perfect. Much more comfortable than the awkward kitchen knife. There was ancient power in the knife. Full of his earth magic and some of this world's magic too. It was a killing knife. He saw visions of it killing many and killing them well. He reached inside it with his thoughts and asked the knife to assist him. It almost seemed as if in that moment, it became a part of his own body in its alliance.

Leaving the apartment, this time without pausing, he made his way back the way he had originally come. Heard the loud apartment and something told him to investigate. Opening the door, he was astonished and disgusted by what he saw. A large hot tub with bubbling water was on the right side of the room, in it sat six people drinking some sort of deep red-colored drink and clearly not sober. Two women and four men. They all were naked and laughing and watching across the room. To the left stood a large bed on which lay a wretched Piggurl on her stomach, arms tied above her head, face turned to the side, squealing in absolute terror and pain as two men held her legs open far too wide and another knelt behind her defiling her. There was blood everywhere and running from her sex. A naked woman lay beside the creature clearly sucking blood from a gaping slash on her arm. Every human was laughing.

Vomit rose in Mark's throat but the lust to kill them all was stronger. It was at this moment that several of the people in the hot tub noticed him standing there. There was alarm in their voices but he heard none of it. He threw the knife at the Piggurl and the blade struck the base of her neck perfectly, killing her instantly. The man who was raping her noticed her instantly limp body and stopped, looking over his shoulder just as Mark threw his hands violently toward him, casting out a thick briar patch with wicked thorns which grew at such a rate and size that the raping man, the two who had been holding her legs and the blood-sucking woman were all encased within it and their screams of surprise turned to terror and pain as the thorns grew to such a size that they all became skewered.

Turning to the hot tub, one of the men had managed to climb out, spilling his half-empty glass of what Mark now realized was blood itself. He snarled in disgust and imagined skewering the man with a javelin and then becoming aware that a sharp living stick grew in his palm, he cocked his arm back and threw with all his might, the planet's spear easily running clear through the man and into the side of the tub, pinning him there like an entomologist's dream. The man's screams of pain rose as the four within the briar patch all suddenly silenced. Blood ran in puddles across the floor. The five remaining people within the hot tub sat motionless. One man had stood but all were frozen in fear. Mark held a finger to his lips and shushed them. The standing man slowly sank back down, shock settling in, as one of the women outright fainted and slid beneath the water. No one bent to help her. The man pinned to the edge of the tub suddenly stopped screaming and fell over as he had no more blood left to give to the growing lake beneath his naked feet.

Mark walked to the bed and the briar patch accommodated him, twisting away as he reached in and removed the earth knife from the Piggurl's neck. Turning back to the others, he stalked forward, purpose in each step. Then in a fury of movement, sprung forward and using the knife's magic, easily severed each of their necks one after the other. Reaching beneath the water's surface, he pulled the drowned woman from the water and slit her neck as well, then spit in her face.

Marching down the hallway, Mark's stomach became iron. So this was how the Piggurls knew of the Keepers. This was how they had got the key fob which he now carried. The praefects were disgusting and vile creatures and not one of them deserved life. They had failed in their duties to their people, they had failed in keeping their word with the planet and its people. These so-called humans had been given their chance. They had made their decisions. Now it was going to be Mark who would take them all down. None of them deserved anything but the worst kind of death and that was just what he would give them.

This was his revolution. He was coming.

END.

Your face is a grimace
and your limbs shake
as the screen's glow of static
casts your features
in a ghastly blue-grey.
Sweet dreams, indeed.

Author Biographies

A.P. CHRISTOPHER writes poetry, short stories, and novels.

Blog: *thepegasusfiasco.com*

— — —

RIVER DIXON has unknowingly found himself trapped in the incessant heat and beauty of Arizona. It is here, along with his family, that he finds solace stringing together words in an attempt to find a structure or sequence that may one day makes sense of all this.

Blog: The Stories In Between at *thestoriesinbetween.com*
Website: *Potter's Grove Press at pottersgrovepress.com*

— — —

ROBERT BIRKHOFER is a writer, a dreamer, and a coffee drinker. He lives in sunny Arizona with his wife and their two cats. Visit Robert's website to read more of his stories and for information on his other published works.

Blog: The Mad Puppeteer at *themadpuppeteer.com*
Instagram: *@the_madpuppeteer*

— — —

AGYANI tries to make others listen, think, and smile and feels that a point can best be driven home through humor. Through his works, he tries to highlight the nuances about people around us which we tend to miss out on.

— — —

LOU RASMUS is a writer from Chicago. His work has been featured by Manic Raven Press, Untwine USA, Silverleaf Poetry, and his debut novel, *Dead Red Fish*, is available on Amazon , along with his book of poetry, *Grapefruit Juice*, and his third novel *Primrose Isle*.

Website: *lourasmus.com*
Instagram: *@lou_rasmus*

BRAEDEN MICHAELS is a married American author living in beautiful Georgia with his family and his own unique creativity. Within his analytical mind dwell the many passages and corners of the world built by observation, investigative perception, and penetrating rationale. He's been published in several anthologies as well as his own books of poetry, written in the method of Deconstructive Literature, in which he pulls apart nuances within human nature then organizes and restores it in a poetic style. You can read more from him on his website, *braedenmichaels.com*.

Blog: Storm of Ink at *braedenmichaels.com*
Instagram: *@braeden_michaels_author*

— — —

M. ENNENBACH is a lot of things. Poet. Writer. Father. Fool. He writes from the heart and emotion that may be strange, raw, or disturbing. He is from Illinois but lives in Texas. His kids are the most important part of his life. His books *Notches, Hunger on the Chisholm Trail, (un)poetic,* and *(un)fettered* can be found at any major book seller.

— — —

MARK RYAN was born in Oxford, growing up in the shadow of the dreaming spires. He studied film at London Metropolitan University, graduating to M.A in Film Theory. His work leans, bends, and sways to the metaphysical and supernatural, with a tendency to dabble in the macabre. Questioning questions and searching for answers in the eye of the storm, where there is always hope.

Blog: Havoc and Consequences at *havocandconsequence.wordpress.com*
X: *@MarkRyan8289*
Website: *markryanhavoc.com*

— — —

TARA CARIBOU is a storyteller at heart. She has three poetry and photographic art books, *Fallen Star Rising, Four,* and *Euphoria in Blue.* An avid reader of hard science fiction and modern poetry, you will most often find her writing short stories and poetry barefoot on some rural Alaskan beach, out in the woods or staring out at the stars, where her heart continually wanders in the cold.

Blog: *taracaribou.com*
Instagram:*@tara_caribou*

www.ingramcontent.com/pod-product-compliance
Lightning Source LLC
Chambersburg PA
CBHW032148020726
47496CB00003B/769